SPENCER COHEN, BOOK TWO

THE SPENCER COHEN SERIES

N.R. WALKER

COPYRIGHT

Cover Artist: Reese Dante
Editor: Boho Edits
Spencer Cohen Series © 2016 N.R. Walker
Publisher: BlueHeart Press
Second Edition: 2023

ALL RIGHTS RESERVED:

This literary work may not be reproduced or transmitted in any form or by any means, including electronic or photographic reproduction, in whole or in part, without express written permission, except in the case of brief quotations embodied in critical articles and reviews.
This is a work of fiction and any resemblance to persons, living or dead, or business establishments, events or locales is coincidental. The Licensed Art Material is being used for illustrative purposes only.

WARNING:

Intended for an 18+ audience only. This book contains material that maybe offensive to some and is intended for a mature, adult audience. It contains graphic language, explicit sexual content, and adult situations.
The author uses Australian English spelling and grammar.

TRADEMARKS:

All trademarks are the property of their respective owners.

DEDICATION

This series is dedicated to every Spencer out there: for those who have lost everything but still have hope, for those too afraid to love again but crave it all the same, for those who have been through hell yet are still strong enough to smile, and for those who wear their scars inked into their skin.

N.R. WALKER

THE SPENCER COHEN

SERIES BOOK TWO

ONE

I was nervous. I was also hungover, but my adrenaline was pumping, my heart was pounding, my palms were sweating, but in that totally exciting, this-is-really-happening kind of way. Andrew looked at me and smiled. "I hope you don't mind that I slept on your couch?"

"No, not at all," I replied quickly. "I'm glad you did. I'm sorry about last night." It was about the fifth time I'd apologised. "I don't normally drink like that."

"Emilio told me," he said. "He came up and knocked on the door to see how you were. You were still asleep, so he told me to come down into the shop. He spent the morning trying to tell me not to be mad at you and that you were one of the good guys."

I looked at the table between us, feeling a little embarrassed that Emilio had gone into bat for me. Andrew had suggested the Moroccan place I'd taken him to before, and without even asking me what I wanted, he ordered what I'd ordered for him once: a full breakfast of pancakes and *khobz b'chehma*, coffee for him, and green tea for me. It filled me with an unfamiliar warmth to know he knew me that well. "Yeah, he and Daniela are good people."

"He said he'd only ever seen you like that once before," Andrew said gently. He kept his hands on the table but slid his foot alongside mine. That simple touch was reassuring, yet such an innocent gesture. My stomach flooded with butterflies. "That it was when your brother turned up? Emilio didn't say anything more than that."

I swallowed hard and gave him a nod. Thankfully Zineb came to the table with our drinks. It gave me a moment to gather my thoughts. Normally I would deflect the question, and for one split second, I thought of calling veto. But Andrew was different. *This* was different. So I took a deep breath, and although I spoke to my green tea, Andrew listened intently.

"I have two brothers, Lewis and Archie. I'm the eldest, and we're all two years apart. My youngest brother, Archie, came to visit last year. It didn't end well." I cleared my throat. "I um, I've been on my own since I was sixteen. My parents kicked me out."

"Because you're gay?"

"Yeah." I looked up at Andrew then to find a look of shock and anger on his face. I gave him a sad smile. "It's funny you know, I had the best childhood. It really was. Great neighbourhood, good friends, we rode our bikes, played sport. Mum and Dad both worked, but they drove me and my brothers around after school to a bunch of different sports and stuff. We did things together as a family, went camping, had holidays up the coast. I thought I could tell my mum anything."

"Oh, Spencer," Andrew whispered. He slid his hand across the table and gave my hand a squeeze. I grabbed hold of his fingers, not wanting to lose that touch, which surprised even me. I hadn't realised how much I'd needed the contact.

"As it turned out, it was probably something I should have kept to myself."

"What happened?"

"Mum went kind of quiet. Dad went off. I'd never seen him so mad," I answered with a shake of my head. "For two days our house was... well, it wasn't a very nice place to be. When I got home from school on the second day my mum sat me down and told me I had to go."

"They what?"

"Yep. My things were already packed. Just some clothes and a few school things out of my room. I couldn't take anything else. Wasn't allowed. And my old man just sat there and never said a bloody word."

Andrew's jaw bulged. "You were sixteen? What did you do?"

I stayed at my friend's place for a week or so. But then my dad put an end to that by telling my mate's parents that maybe I'd corrupt their son, and I couldn't stay there anymore. Spent a few nights in the park before my aunty heard and took me in."

Andrew took a deep breath and his nostrils flared. "I am so pissed off for you right now."

"I survived. Actually, I was kind of lucky."

"Lucky?"

"That I had my Aunt Marvie. She took me in and loved me like a son. She was the only family I had. Actually, she wasn't my aunty; she was my dad's aunty, so technically she was my great-aunt Marvie."

"Was?"

"She passed away last year," I said quietly, swallowing down the lump in my throat. "I didn't even know she was sick. Apparently she had been for a while—she would have known when I'd made plans to travel here, and she was all for me to go. She never told me she was sick. She wouldn't have wanted me to worry. In fact, she was excited for me when I told her I wanted to travel. She gave me some money and told me to have the time of my life." I sighed. "I only found out she passed away weeks later when the solicitor contacted me about her will. I'd been here for a few months."

Andrew paled and a wave of sadness washed over his face. "Oh man. Spencer, I'm sorry."

"Me too." I sipped my tea and took a moment to get my thoughts in order. It wasn't easy to talk about this, but it seemed the last few days had reopened the wounds I'd thought I'd managed to heal. I took a shaky breath. "Anyway, I'd been living with Aunt Marvie for about four years—I could have moved out, but she was kinda old and she liked the company, and to be honest, I loved living with her. Anyway, it was my dad's fiftieth. It was a big party, black tie, that kind of thing. I mean, I wasn't surprised that I wasn't invited. I expected nothing less. But he told Aunt Marvie she wasn't welcome either, and there was a huge family fight. God, my grandmother cried for a week." I shrugged. "Nan was torn between her sister and her son. I mean, it was just awful. Apparently Dad blamed me for the whole thing. Said it was all my fault because *if I didn't choose to be gay*," I imitated his voice, "*then none of this would have happened.*"

Zineb put our food on the table, and obviously detecting the seriousness of our conversation, she didn't offer anything else but a kind smile.

"Anyway," I continued, "he told me that in no uncertain terms they now thought of me as dead."

Andrew's mouth fell open, and without taking his eyes off me, he slowly put his fork on the table.

"But what hurt the most was not being told Aunt Marvie died. That was low. I mean, I would've gone to her funeral… I don't even know if she had one." I blinked back those all-telling tears that Andrew had seen too much of in the last two days. I laughed them off. "Man, you must think I'm a blubbering idiot. I haven't cried this much in, well, over a year."

He shook his head and squeezed my hand. "Not at all. My God, Spencer, I can't believe how horrible this is. And then your brother turned up here?"

I nodded. "I hadn't seen him in years. He's four years younger than me, so I guess we weren't that close. I left home when he was twelve, and only saw him a few times in the six years I spent with Aunt Marvie. Anyway, he was here on an end-of-college trip, or so he said. I had no clue he was even coming until he turned up." I gave Andrew a sad smile. "It's funny how hope never really goes away. I thought for a second it could be good, you know? But it, well it wasn't. He gave me what was basically a cease and desist letter from my dad's attorney. I was to never make contact with them again. See, I'd called them about Aunt Marvie and well, apparently my father didn't like that. There's other legal stuff about the family business as well, but yeah, basically I'm to never contact them again."

Andrew sat there, staring at me with his jaw slack and a flush across his cheeks I think might have been from anger. He stabbed a pancake with his fork. "If it's all right with you, I think I'd like to hate your family."

That made me laugh. "You can take a number. That list is long."

"They really did that to you?"

I nodded. "My brother didn't know what was in the letter. Well, he said he didn't, but it doesn't matter. I don't blame him for not wanting anything to do with me. He was pretty young when my parents would have brainwashed him, or whatever they did. And I don't doubt my father made him give the letter to me just to hurt me. He could have just had his solicitor mail it."

"Have you spoken to him since?"

"No. The solicitor's letter was pretty clear. It was basically to cut me out of their money. Aunt Marvie left me a fair chunk of cash when she passed away, so I think my parents just wanted to be sure that didn't happen again when they die. Aunt Marvie had it written in her will that my father couldn't contest her final wishes because he was a bitter homophobic bastard," I said with a laugh.

Andrew smiled at that. "She sounds like she was an amazing lady."

"She was," I replied simply. "Thank you for saying that."

"I'm so sorry you had such an awful time. I can't even imagine going through that."

"It's hard to know you're alone. Like really alone. Sometimes I think it would have been better if they'd died, you know? Like *really* died, in a car accident or something. I'd have closure that way at least. But to be not-wanted, yeah, that was hard."

Andrew sat back in his seat and sighed. "I had no idea. Though I knew something had happened. Your eyes flinched when I mentioned family, and then you vetoed my question about your tattoos."

"And I thought I hid it well."

Andrew smiled, though it was brief. "And I made you watch *How To Train Your Dragon 2*, and the dad died. God, Spencer I am so sorry."

"You weren't to know," I told him. "And to be honest, it kind of blindsided me. I wasn't expecting it, and I just got barrelled. I didn't mean to freak on you like that. If I'm being completely honest, I'd been out of sorts all week. You know, some cute guy I was supposed to be working for was doing my head in. I'd spent years not allowing myself to feel anything, and then this guy from the cover of *Sexiest Geek Alive* knocked me on my arse."

"Oh," Andrew mumbled quietly. It took him a second to realise I was talking about him. "*Oh.*"

"I'd told myself years ago that I'd never let anyone get close enough to hurt me again," I admitted quietly. "I have kept myself at a distance from any kind of relationship. But then there was you."

Andrew blushed and gave me a shy smile.

I had to say this now, or I never would. "And I have to admit Andrew, it scared the hell outta me. I kept thinking I could see myself with you, and that went against everything I'd spent years telling myself. I never wanted to put myself out there, ya know? But then I realised when I left you there with Eli, that I already had. And I thought you chose him, and I was unwanted all over again. So my head was all over the place, with you and my family. I don't know if that explains why I lost my shit last night, but that's all I've got."

He looked right at me. "It more than explains it. And you are not unwanted, just so you know. Quite the opposite. You were on the cover of *Trendy Living in LA*, were you not?"

I smiled at his attempt to make me feel better, and it was a nice change from the heavy topic of conversation. "Come on, dig in. Or it'll get cold, and then Zineb will yell Arabic at us for not liking her food." I waited for him to have a few bites. "I promise I won't lose my shit on you again."

He chuckled around his mouthful of pancake. "Can I ask you something?"

I wasn't sure what else there was to say. "Sure."

"You never wanted me to get back with Eli?"

I put my fork down and sipped my tea. Here it was. All or nothing. "No. I didn't. When you stayed with him in the bar, I thought it was what you wanted. I mean, it was what we worked at. But I hoped. And hope was something I hadn't allowed myself to feel for a while, I guess. And you know, that dreaded hope can be a dangerous thing. I mean, you were different. From day one, you weren't like any other guy I'd worked for." I huffed out a laugh. It was so ridiculous to say this stuff out loud. "And I tried to keep it all separate, but I couldn't because you see, I have a stupid heart, and a stupid brain, and then we kissed."

Andrew smiled the eye-crinkling kind of smile. "And by God, you can kiss," he said. This time it was me who blushed, which he clearly found amusing, or appealing, or possibly both. "And just so you know, it was what did it for me."

"Kissing me?"

Andrew nodded, and he cleared his throat. "I thought I was fooling myself, thinking we, you know, you could ever be interested in me. I mean, I thought I wanted Eli back, which I can see now was not what I wanted at all. When he left I was missing something. I wanted *something*, I just didn't know what it was. But it was never Eli. God, you made me realise he didn't know the first thing about me. And then you kissed me and..." he flushed a full shade of red up his neck, "...and I thought that can't be part of the act, right?"

I shook my head slowly. "I wasn't acting." I shifted in my seat. "In fact, I don't think I ever was with you."

He pushed his empty plate away and bit his lip. "So we're seeing if this goes somewhere? You know, just so we're on the same page. It doesn't have to be anything official. I just want to spend time with you." He frowned. "I tend to get ahead of myself, so if I'm reading this wrong..."

My chest suddenly felt too small for my heart. I let out a

nervous laugh. "You aren't reading this wrong. I just wanna spend time with you too. And I know it's only early days, but just so you know, I'm not opposed to *official*." Then I shrugged. "I'm not overly familiar with it either, but if we're gonna do this, we may as well do it properly, yeah?"

His smile was really something special. Then he looked around the café and waved over Zineb. "I think we need to leave," he told me. "I need you to kiss me again, and I don't think we should do that here."

I barked out a laugh, and he looked up as Zineb arrived at our table. "Check please."

TWO

WE GOT BUSTED AT THE STAIRS THAT LED TO MY FLAT. I'd suggested we avoid the knowing looks and smirks from everyone in the shop and go straight around the back. But Gabe was there having a cigarette and wore a shit-eating grin when he saw us. "Going upstairs for anything in particular? You boys look like you're in a hurry."

Andrew stopped and stuffed his hands in his pockets and kind of hid behind me waiting for me to speak. I deadpanned, "Yeah, I feel much better now, thanks for asking."

Gabe snorted and nodded to my apartment. "About to feel a whole lot better, I'd guess."

Andrew gently pushed me toward the stairs, following close behind. He cleared his throat. "Gee, I'd really love to stay and chat."

Gabe laughed, and I let myself be ushered up the first few steps, when we heard Lola. "Gabe, who you talking to, honey?"

Gabe madly waved his hand up toward my door which meant go-go-go. "Get outta here before she sees you," he whisper-shouted. Then he turned back inside the shop. "No one, babe. Just mumbling to myself."

I took the stairs two at a time with Andrew on my heels, and by the time I got the key into the lock and we fell through the doorway, Lola called out, "I saw you Spencer! Gabe, what the hell?"

"Just giving my brothers a chance, babe," Gabe answered. "Boys gotta look out for each other."

"I owe you, man," I yelled back before I closed the door behind us with a laugh.

Then it was just me and Andrew. And that made me incredibly nervous. I was already breathless. My smile kinda slid away, and I wiped my hands on my thighs. "Can I get you a drink?"

"Sure," he said. I thought he might go into the living room, but he didn't. He followed me to the kitchen. I mean, my apartment wasn't big, but in that moment it felt claustrophobic. Like I could feel the heat of his body no matter where he stood.

I handed him a bottle of water and took a mouthful from mine to give myself a moment to get my hammering heart under control. But then Andrew licked his lips, leaving them pink and glistening, and then I lost all signal to my brain.

He put the bottle down on the counter at my side and stood right in front of me. He was close but not quite touching, and so in control, whereas I was breathing like I'd run a marathon. Andrew smiled and put his fingers to my chin and ran his thumb across my beard. He leaned in so close I could feel the warmth of his breath. "About that kiss..."

He slid his hand along my jaw and held my head, right where he wanted it. He brushed his lips against mine, almost but not quite, and I thought my knees would buckle. My heart was pounding so loud I think he could hear it. Then he touched his bottom lip to mine before pulling back just a fraction. My breath hitched, and he smiled. "My favourite part is the almost-kiss," he whispered. "It's intoxicating."

He was using big words and complete sentences while my head was spinning in circles, and when he nudged his nose to mine, all I could come out with was, "I have a stupid brain."

Andrew laughed, and I well and truly ruined the moment. Not that he seemed too fazed because he took my face in both hands and pressed his lips to mine. He opened his mouth and tilted my head, and when our tongues met, pure desire exploded in my blood.

I pulled him closer and kissed him harder, finally—*finally*—feeling him against me, tasting his mouth, drinking him in. He was heaven. This was what I wanted. *Him.* To kiss him like this whenever I wanted. I could feel his surprise at how fiercely I kissed him, but he soon relaxed in my arms and met me with equal fervour.

I could feel his entire front against me, and I had no doubt he could feel how hard I was. Knowing he had the same reaction to me spurred me on, and I couldn't help but grind my hips into his.

He moaned into the kiss, and the sound went straight to my cock. I pulled our mouths apart and pushed him back just a little, putting some space between us. He looked confused so I kept my hands fisted in his shirt. "Don't go too far," I whispered, while trying to get my breath. I licked the corner of my mouth, and he watched my tongue. His pupils were blown, his lips swollen, and he looked so fucking hot. "Just need a second," I told him.

He put his palm to my cheek. "Do you need some time?"

I laughed, embarrassed. "Only if you don't want this to be over in about ten seconds."

"Oh." His eyes widened. "*Oh.*"

"Yeah, sorry. It's been a while for me, and you're ridiculously hot."

Andrew laughed and ran one hand through his hair. "Well, the first kiss certainly wasn't a fluke."

"Apparently not." I snorted, and my brain finally found its voice. "We should um, we should take a breather, I guess. I mean, we didn't talk about anything physical. Do you have expectations or limitations? Do you want to take it slow? I mean, you only broke up with whatshisname a month ago. I don't want you to feel pressured…"

"Are you asking me what I want?"

"Yeah, I guess. I mean, we've been dating for—oh, are we even dating? Is that what we are?"

Andrew grinned. "I'm not opposed to that."

A herd of butterflies took flight in my belly. "Right. Okay then. So, we've been dating for like two hours."

Andrew took my hand and ran his thumb over my knuckles. A smirk played at his lips. "Well, technically, we've been fake-dating for two weeks."

"True."

"We've been out for dinner, breakfast, drinks," he said. There was a hint of daring in his voice. "So, two weeks is actually a decent amount of time before we even kissed, right?"

"True."

"Actually two weeks is a decent amount of time for other first things, right?"

I liked where he was going with this. "If you say so."

He pulled on my hand and started to walk backwards, leading me forwards, to my bedroom. "I say so."

"Are you sure?"

He stopped walking. "I am, whenever you are. Are *you* sure?"

"I am *so* sure."

He smiled, relieved. "Oh, thank God." He pulled my hand so I was flush against him, and that adrenaline, liquid fire lit up my blood once more. He feathered his lips over mine. "It doesn't have to be sex," he said gruffly. Then he pulled our hips together so our erections pressed against each other. "But we can get rid of these, yes?"

And that was all the encouragement I needed. "Fuck yes." I pushed him backwards and into my room with my mouth planted on his. My hands went to his hips, and when the backs of his legs hit my bed, I pushed him again, letting him fall onto his back. I crawled over him, admiring the bulge tenting his trousers.

It made my mouth water.

He leaned up a little and pulled his shirt over his head and lay back again. He was kinda pale, but all those hours in the gym left him trim and toned. The sight literally stole my breath. "You're so fucking hot."

Without taking his eyes off me, he put his hands to his trousers and slowly popped the button.

I leaned back on my knees so I could take a second to simmer down, but it was no use. Instead, I palmed my dick. "Jesus, Andrew, this is going to be over embarrassingly fast."

He bit his lip like my statement was a challenge and slid his fingers underneath his briefs. He gripped himself and I saw the engorged head of his dick.

I closed my eyes and took a deep breath. "Oh, fuck."

Then he let go of his dick and used both hands to throw me onto my back on the bed. His strength surprised me, his assertiveness and want for control even more so. He was between my legs and pulled roughly at my jeans, popping the button fly open in one go. Then he was pulling my shirt over my head—he was doing whatever the fuck he wanted with me, and I was letting him.

This was bossy Andrew. Sure, he was quiet, a little shy even, but he had no qualms whatsoever in saying what he thought or asking for what he wanted. Or just taking it. When Andrew had said he was versatile, I might have doubted his topping ability. Well, I certainly didn't doubt him now.

"You're gonna make me come," I grated out.

He leaned over me, pushing my legs apart with his thighs, and slid his free hand around my aching cock. He spoke gruffly, with his lips almost touching mine. "Don't fight it."

With both hands, I pulled his mouth to mine. With his hand pumping me and his weight on top of me, his tongue in my mouth, I couldn't hold it back anymore.

Pleasure exploded low in my belly, hot and delicious. My back arched as my orgasm rocked through me, come smearing our bellies. When I opened my eyes, Andrew was above me, watching me with wonder in his eyes. "Fuck," he whispered.

It was the first time I'd ever heard him swear, and it made me laugh. Or maybe it was the orgasm-induced haze in my brain that made me laugh. Either way, he leaned down and kissed me softly, slowly. He brought his hand up, and resting on his elbows, he put both hands in my hair. I wanted to tell him I think he just put jizz in my hair, but he rubbed his cock against me again and again, faster and faster until he broke the kiss so he could groan. He bucked one last time and stilled, his hot come shooting between us.

I had never seen anything like it.

He slumped down on me, boneless and spent, so I rolled

us over until I was on top of him. I kissed his lips, his cheek, his jaw, down his neck to his collarbone, and I smiled. "I was right," I told him. "That blush goes from your cheeks to your chest."

He let out a laugh, and his arm fell heavily back to the bed.

"It's incredibly sexy," I told him, nipping the pink-flushed skin of his jaw. "You are incredibly sexy."

He opened one eye lazily and looked at me like I'd lost my mind. "Right." He closed his eyes again and shook his head.

I kissed him softly. "Look at me." I waited until his eyes opened. They took a second to focus and I fought a smile, but I kept my face just inches from his so he *had* to look at me. "You are the sexiest guy I've ever met. You're intelligent, talented, funny, and you made me come in a matter of minutes."

He blushed again and tried to look away. I gently put my fingers to his chin and kept eye contact. "You're a remarkable guy, Andrew. I'll just have to keep telling you that until you believe me."

He stared, just stared at me, and I couldn't have looked away even if I wanted to. Finally he cleared his throat and smirked. "Now, I'm not strictly opposed to staying here all day with you, but maybe we could shower? We're a bit, you know..."

"Sticky?"

Andrew chuckled. "Uh, yeah. And our clothes are a mess. Well, actually, it was your shirt."

I pecked his lips and rolled off him. "I liked that shirt on you too," I said, offering him my hand to pull him off the bed. "I think we might need a trip to the laundromat."

"I have a washing machine at my place," he replied. "We could just go there."

I looked at my bed. "My sheets are a mess too."

He glanced at the rumpled bedding and shrugged. "Well, if they need washing, we could make sure they *really* need washing."

I laughed at that. "Are you suggesting something?"

He ran his hand up my arm, across my chest, and up to my jaw, where he gently scratched my beard. "I am suggesting something, yes," he whispered. He pulled my chin between his thumb and finger and drew me in for a kiss. "I think we should shower first."

"Together?"

"Yes."

Wow. "Okay."

He slid his free hand down my stomach and over my still-open fly and palmed my half-hard dick. "Is this okay?"

I groaned out a laugh. "Ah, yes. Very okay."

He licked his lips, and my eyes trained in on his tongue. He gave me a squeeze. "How big is your shower?"

Instead of answering, I grabbed his hand and led him to the bathroom. The shower wasn't huge, but I didn't care; we were both fitting in it. I turned the taps on, then turned to face him. He was still shirtless, and his trousers were undone. I could see the bulge barely concealed in his briefs. "Fuck, that's hot," I murmured. I stood against him, our fronts completely touching, and I whispered against his lips, "And you have a dirty mouth."

He smirked. "It's always the quiet ones..."

Smiling, I kissed him and slid my hands over his hips and pushed his trousers down. Then I cupped his balls and watched as his eyes swam and his breath hitched. I kissed him, his mouth open and willing. He wrapped his arms around me and slid his hands over my arse, pushing my jeans and briefs down in one go.

It was different being naked in front of Andrew. I was almost nervous, which was a new thing for me. It was like I was stripped of more than just clothes—like he saw *me*.

He was glorious naked. He was well-defined and well-hung. He was circumcised and a good many inches long, hanging proudly from a nest of blond pubic hair. The skin over his chest, stomach, and arms was flawless. Not a mark, not a scar, just pale and perfect.

His eyes scanned over my body, my tattooed arms, bare chest, and down to my cock. When his eyes met mine again, he looked a little drunk. I chuckled at him and stepped into the shower.

"Something funny?" he asked, following me into the cubicle.

I soaped up my chest and washed the dried come from my stomach. "Not at all." I let my head fall back in the stream of hot water and quickly washed my face before handing him the soap. Only when I opened my eyes, he was on his knees and the water was streaming over him as he looked up at me. "Oh, Jesus."

"It's not funny now, is it?"

I laughed anyway and leaned my back against the tiles but kept my hips were they were. "God, Andrew."

"Is it okay if I taste you?" he asked, his voice gruff.

Oh, fuck. My belly tightened at his words. "Do I have to beg?"

He put his fist around the base of my length, and I made the mistake of looking down at him. Because, fuck. The head of my cock was at his lips, and his eyes were dark, his skin was wet and his tongue... oh God, his tongue felt like heaven when he licked me.

I softly threaded my fingers through his hair. Not guiding

or urging. I just needed to touch him. Then he took me into his mouth, and my stupid brain short-circuited.

He kept one hand around my shaft, the other cupped my balls, and his mouth worked the head. And he sucked my orgasm right out of me.

Jesus. Fucking. Christ.

My head spun, and I saw stars behind my eyes. Then his hands were on my face, and he kissed me. It was a mix of water and the taste of me, and then he was shutting the water off. I was still lightheaded when I stepped out of the shower, but I couldn't miss his erection. I dried off quickly and wrapped a towel around me, and even as he was still towelling himself off, I snatched up his hand and led him back to the bedroom. "Your turn," I told him. "Lay down."

He sat on the bed and scooted back. Then he propped up the pillows and leaned back, adjusting them so he was almost sitting up. "What?" he asked when I laughed at him. "I want to watch."

I knelt on the bed and edged up between his open legs. He truly was gorgeous. I wasted no time in returning the favour. I lifted his heavy cock and licked from his sac up to the head, eliciting a hiss from him.

When I tasted his slit, his breath hitched, and then he moaned when I took him into my mouth. He was so vocal, every reaction was a reward for my efforts, and it spurred me on. As much as I wanted to prolong it, to draw out every sound from his lips, I wanted to taste him even more.

His hands found purchase in my hair, and he had no qualms in showing me how he liked it. *Fuck.* And when I looked up at him, he was biting his bottom lip, and his chest was heaving. His eyes were smouldering and locked on where his cock disappeared into my mouth.

"Oh, God," he ground out. "I'm gonna come."

I sucked harder and pumped his shaft until he flexed under me and shot into my throat with a raspy cry. His whole body shuddered and jerked as his orgasm swept through him, and only when he slumped back onto the pillows and squirmed did I release him.

I kissed his nipple, which made him chuckle, and then his lips, which made him hum. I grabbed the bedcovers and pulled them up and lay down beside him in the nest of pillows he'd made himself. He snuggled in, I put my arm around him, and with just a few deep breaths between us, we dozed.

It had been a really long time since I'd lain in bed and just slept with a man. Normally I only ever spent time in bed with a guy for sex and sex only, but this was... nice.

Really, really fucking nice.

It was warm and comforting and safe.

It was hard to get my head around the fact I didn't even know this man two weeks ago. Even more so, that up until yesterday, I was still trying to get him back with his ex. Not that I was trying overly hard—it was the last thing I actually wanted. God, I wanted him for myself, and here he was in my bed. In my arms.

And it all started because he paid me to get him back with his ex, and I wondered if the exchange of money made this weird.

Like he could read my mind, he said, "Um, about the contract..."

I sighed. "Can we just rip it up?"

He lifted his head up and looked at me. "I still owe you money."

I barked out a laugh. "Ah, no you don't. In fact, I think I should give you back what you paid me already."

He shook his head. "No, you don't need to do that."

"I'd feel better if I did," I told him honestly.

"But you did your job. Everything you planned to happen, did."

"I didn't *plan* for you to pick me," I corrected gently. "I *wanted* you to."

He chuckled. "Wrong word choice, sorry. But you still did your job."

"I can't take your money."

"Spencer, you still have bills to pay, food to eat."

"I'd feel… wrong, if I took it." I cringed.

His eyebrows furrowed. "Why?"

"I dunno," I hedged. "Like a rent-boy or something."

Andrew's mouth fell open. "Oh, Spencer. No."

"Yep," I grinned at him. "A rent-boy, paid for services rendered."

"What does that make me?"

"My pimp."

He laughed. "Gee, thanks."

I snorted. "Better being the pimp than the hooker, I guess."

He made a thoughtful face. "Depends. At least the hooker gets laid."

I cracked up laughing. "And to think you said Eli wasn't too interested in sex. I'm starting to think the man was crazy."

Andrew was quiet then, and I wondered if I'd said the wrong thing. "Well, it kind of makes sense if his whole agenda for living with me was to take the original prints."

"He said he didn't, though, right?"

"Yeah."

"Do you believe him?"

"Funnily enough, I do. He was genuine when he admitted that."

"How was he, last night?" I asked. "When you told him."

"He wasn't too surprised, I don't think. He looked disappointed."

"So he should be."

"He said he'd seen us together before, that time at the bar for his friend's birthday." He sighed. "The whole thing is a bit of a mess, but to be honest, I'm glad it ended the way it did because I got to meet you."

I gave him a bit of a squeeze. "Me too."

"He also said you went and saw him at his work. He recognized you."

I had told Andrew I'd gone to see Eli, but that wasn't my concern. "Did he think it was suspicious? Did you tell him you hired me? You know, in the beginning?"

He surprised me by laughing. "Good Lord, no. Why would I do that? He just figured you were curious about him."

I leaned up so I could see his face and told him the truth. "I was. I wanted to see what kind of guy I was dealing with, in a situation that didn't involve you. And I had to see what he was like," I admitted. "And if I'm being completely honest, I wanted to see why you picked him."

Andrew gave me a smug smirk. He looked kinda sleepy and sated. Happy, even. "I didn't pick him. He picked me. Well, to begin with anyway."

"So, he's not *that* crazy." I didn't want to ask if Eli admitted to singling Andrew out in hopes of stealing his artwork—the thought alone made me ragey—and I didn't want Andrew to feel used. Any more than he already did, anyway. "He's still a wanker. But you have a history with him, and I can respect that."

"Can we not talk about him?" he asked. He ran his hand through my hair and then studied my eyes for a moment. "I'd much prefer to talk about you. And if we don't get up off this bed soon, I don't think we'll be getting up all day."

The thought alone of what he was implying made me hum. "Gee, tough decision. To do my laundry or you." He laughed at that, but rolled off the bed making me fall face-first into my pillow. I groaned. "Laundry it is then."

THREE

"Can today involve a nap?" I asked in the car on our way to his place.

"Are you five?"

I rubbed my eyes with the heels of my hands. "Last night is catching up with me."

"Or are you just trying to get me back into bed?"

"Possibly. Do you always answer every question with a question?"

He grinned. "Possibly."

"I really am sorry about last night. I actually don't drink that often," I told him. "Which is why I was so wrecked."

"It's okay Spencer," he said, looking from the road to me. He smiled. "Emilio told me that you're not a real drinker. Maybe a few beers now and then, but not normally hard liquor." He laughed a bit. "I think they were worried I'd think less of you. They were all so busy telling me what a good guy you are."

I shook my head. "I didn't ask them to do that."

"Yes, I know. They were worried about you."

I sighed. "I owe them a pretty big thank you. Dinner or something."

"They also told me you'd been different with me from day one," he said, just all casual-like. There was a hint of humour in his eyes.

"They did, huh?"

"Yep. Said you were all ridiculous smiles whenever you mentioned my name."

"Right, then. Well, I'm taking back the offer to buy them dinner."

He laughed. "So it's true?"

"My answer depends on whether you agree to a nap this afternoon."

He laughed. "I take it that's a yes."

I could feel my cheeks flush with embarrassment. "I told you already you were different. But I object to the term *ridiculous smiles.*"

He was still smirking when he parked his car near his apartment. I grabbed my bag of laundry from the backseat and followed him inside. "I don't know, Spencer," he said, putting his keys and wallet on the hallstand. His voice was quieter, more serious. "I happened to like hearing that you thought I was special from day one. When they told me, Lola laughed and said my smile matched your ridiculous one. So we're probably even."

I stood there, holding my bag of laundry, not sure what to do with it. I was suddenly nervous. Here we were, alone at his place. I mean, we'd been alone all morning, but this was somehow different. It was like we were one breath away from going at it like rabbits, or he was about to tell me he'd changed his mind. "Well, that's good then. We can be ridiculous together."

He studied me for a long moment before walking slowly

over to stand in front of me. He put his hand on my laundry bag, where I was clutching it tightly. His fingers touched mine, and warmth shot up my arm causing the butterflies in my stomach to take flight, and he stared into my eyes. I licked my lips, wanting to kiss him, and he leaned in just a fraction, but stopped short of contact. "I'll take that for you," he said gruffly and pulled the bag out of my hand. He took a step back and my breath left me in a rush.

"Fuck," I mumbled, not really meaning to say the word out loud. "Are you trying to kill me?"

He grinned. "Just checking it wasn't some kind of fluke before."

"A fluke? What fluke? That I find you insanely hot or that you make my stupid brain malfunction?"

He laughed quietly. "Maybe both."

"Well, you could have just asked me," I said, adjusting my now aching—thanks to him—dick.

He watched my hand on my crotch, and his nostrils flared, a rush of pink crept down his neck. His voice cracked when he said, "We better start this laundry."

He turned and walked down the hall past the bathroom, to what I assumed was the laundry, so I followed. He upended the bag, the contents spilling onto the tiled floor.

"Here, I can do that," I told him. "I don't expect you or anyone else to do my washing." I picked up a shirt and moved it to one side and shoved the sheets to the other side. And as I sorted the dark and light coloured clothes, I could feel him watching me. I looked up and smiled. "What?"

"You sort laundry," he said quietly.

"Of course I do. By colour and then fabric."

A slow smile spread across his face, and he bit his lip.

"Do you have a laundry kink I don't know about?" I asked.

He laughed. "Uh no. It's just that I always sort that way too, colour then by types of fabric. Eli never did, and it used to drive me insane." He shrugged. "I like that you do."

"Um, if you like it, then I'm pretty sure it falls in the kink category."

He laughed, a low warm sound, before collecting the sheets off the floor and throwing them in the washing machine. He added powder and set it going, which left us standing close together with nothing between us, and suddenly the air was electric in the small room. I could see the rise and fall of his chest, the heat in his eyes.

Fuck.

There was a chemistry between us that I'd never felt with anyone else. And before my brain could catch up, I slid my hand along his jaw and drew his mouth to mine. He pulled our hips together, slid his arms around me, and it felt so good.

It felt so right.

Andrew tilted his head and deepened the kiss, and I pushed him up against the washing machine, pressing us together.

He was hard, as was I, and our cocks rubbed through the fabric of our pants. He ran his hands over my arse and pulled us closer still, and I moaned without shame.

And just when I was wondering if we should move to the bedroom—I didn't want our first fuck to be on the laundry floor—his phone rang, startling us. He smiled into our kiss and pulled away, leaving the both of us breathless. His eyes were dark, his lips were swollen, and his cheeks were flushed. I decided right then it was my favourite look on him.

He pulled his phone from his pocket, showed me who was calling, and answered. "Sarah?"

Not wanting to lose the moment, I leaned in and kissed his neck. He smelled so good, and he tasted even better. I pressed against him, humming when our bodies aligned so perfectly.

"Really?" he asked, flustered. "Now? Can't it wait?" I heard the buzz of her voice but not the words exactly, and with a frustrated groan, he disconnected the call. "My sister is on her way."

"How long have we got?" I whispered, kissing up to his ear.

"She just walked past my car, so she knows I'm home," he answered breathily, clearly he liked to be kissed there.

Wait. What? I pulled back. "She's here? Now?"

He snorted out a laugh and nodded. "With the worst sense of timing."

I stepped back and palmed my rock hard dick. "Oh man. Talk about awkward."

Andrew did the same to his own erection and hissed. "Tell me about it."

A knock sounded at the door, and Andrew let his head fall back with a groan. "Think horrible thoughts, think horrible thoughts," he mumbled to himself, trying to will his hard-on away as he walked out to answer the front door.

"Yeah, like being interrupted in what was possibly the hottest kiss I've ever had," I added.

Andrew laughed as he opened the door, and Sarah barrelled in. She didn't see me, she hadn't taken her eyes off her brother yet. "Tell me what happened?" she asked him. "I was going to call, but I wasn't far away and I thought I'd get all the details in person. So tell me, what happened last night?"

"Well," Andrew said slowly, as he closed the door behind her. Then he gave a pointed nod to where I was standing against the hall door.

Sarah followed his line of sight. "Hi," I said, giving her a bit of a wave.

Her grin was immediate, as was her relief. "Oh, thank God!" She turned back to Andrew and hugged him. "I'm so glad. I knew! I just knew! When I saw how you two were together at dinner the other night, I just knew!" Sarah let go of Andrew and turned to me. "Oh wait, does you being here mean what I think it means?" she asked. She turned back to look at Andrew. "I mean, what about Eli?"

"Eli's history," Andrew answered. "And yes, this means what you think it means, but well, we think it does." He looked at me and cringed. "We're still working out the details."

"We are," I agreed. "Though I do believe the term *officially dating* was used?"

Andrew smiled at me. "Yeah, I think it was."

"Aww, boyfriends," Sarah said. "That's so cute!" Then she straightened up and looked squarely at her brother. "Tell me everything."

"I'll just go to the bathroom," I said, excusing myself to leave. It was really just an obvious ruse for them to have a few minutes without me. Sure, it also gave me some time to make sure I wasn't sporting a hard-on while talking to his sister. Having her interrupt was a mood killer for sure, and after I'd splashed some cold water on my face and my dick had relaxed enough for me to take a piss, I went back out.

Their conversation was hushed and coming from the kitchen, so I followed the sound. I could smell coffee brewing and found three empty cups on the counter alongside Andrew and Sarah in deep conversation. "...I slept on his couch," Andrew said. The conversation stopped cold when I walked in.

I figured I should contribute to the story. "Yes, I got absolutely shitfaced because I thought I'd lost him to that wanker ex-boyfriend," I said. There was no point in being embarrassed about it. "Andrew tracked me down, found me in a drunken state, sobbing like a baby, and put me to bed. We talked this morning, and now we're here."

Andrew grinned at me before looking at his sister. "Yep. That's pretty much how it went. His friends came and got me this morning and spent an hour trying to convince me to give him a chance."

"Really?" she asked. "They did that?"

Andrew nodded and half-shrugged. "I was already going to. Give him a chance, that is," he said. "I mean, why would I have followed him home if I weren't interested?"

I looked at Sarah. "And for what it's worth, I've never bought anyone else a record player."

Sarah laughed just as the coffee machine beeped. Andrew poured two cups of coffee and stopped short on the third. "Shit. You don't drink coffee, and I don't have any tea."

"Coffee's fine," I told him. "Actually, I probably need a coffee. This hangover is starting to dig its heels in."

Andrew frowned. "If you want to go lie down, just say so."

"Later," I said, taking the cup. The truth was, I didn't really like coffee, but I figured any type of caffeine would help clear the mud in my head. And more importantly, if I was going to lie down on his bed, I certainly didn't want to do that alone.

Sarah sipped her coffee. "So, was Eli really going to take your prints?"

Andrew sighed. "I don't know. I think he was originally, yes. Whether it was his sole intention from the beginning, I just don't know. Actually, I'd rather not know at all. I just want to move on, ya know?"

Sarah nodded slowly, but there was warmth in her smile.

"Well, I'm glad it worked out. And Andrew, my dear brother, you owe me big time."

"What for?"

"I was the one who lined this up, remember?" she motioned between me and Andrew. "You didn't want to even meet Spencer in the beginning."

Andrew looked at me, smiled, and shrugged. "True."

I pretended to be offended.

Sarah snorted. "Oh, Spencer you should have seen him. When we left the café after meeting you the first time, he was all panicky. 'He's too sexy for me. Eli will know it's a set-up because there's no way a guy like that would pick me, blah blah blah.'"

I laughed at her impression of him, and Andrew rolled his eyes. "I'm not embarrassed," he said, his blush proof to the contrary.

"Yes, I do have to wonder why on earth he doesn't see himself the way I do," I said. I waited for Andrew's eyes to meet mine. "Because if I seem to recall, he was on the cover of *Sexy Nerds*, whereas all I managed was page twelve of *Trendy LA*."

Andrew laughed. "It wasn't page twelve. It was page four."

"You were on the cover!"

"I amended yours to the cover," he said, grinning now. "And I even drew your cover. Where's the artwork for my cover?"

"Believe me, you don't want me to draw you anything. I can't even get stick figures right."

Sarah was laughing along with us but was obviously confused. "What are you two talking about?"

"Never mind," Andrew said, sipping his coffee with smiling lips.

"Well then," Sarah said, finishing her coffee. "I'll be going.

Spencer, you have no idea how happy I am to see you here today. I was thinking I was going to turn up and smarmy Eli would be here." She leaned up and kissed my cheek, which was a surprise, but lovely all the same. "Andrew, walk me out?"

Even I knew that was code for "Can I see you in private?".

I didn't mind. If she needed to talk to him without my being there, I had no qualms with that. It just meant, given how honest she'd been about everything else, I wouldn't have liked what she had to say. I took one more sip of coffee and tipped the rest out in the sink. I'd managed half a cup, and that would do me in the coffee department for a while. I didn't know if my head was better or worse for drinking it. Give me green tea any day.

I washed the coffee cups and was drying them when Andrew came back in. "Everything okay?" I asked.

"Oh sure," he said. "She just wanted to lecture me."

"On what?"

"On not screwing this up."

"What on earth could you do to screw this up?"

He shrugged. "She says I rush into things. Which I do, I guess. Like I did with Eli. She just wants me to take a step back and not, you know, move in together after two months of dating and get engaged after six months. That kind of thing."

Well shit. "Do you think we're rushing into anything?"

He shrugged again. "No, but I didn't think I was with Eli either. But in hindsight I did, so maybe she has a point. We have technically only been together for a few hours."

I laughed at that. "Well, when you put it like that."

One corner of his mouth pulled down. "Even though we fake-dated for two weeks."

"I totally count that, by the way," I told him. "Those two

weeks were awesome. And even though we didn't meet in a very conventional way, I don't regret it. I mean, I regret that you were hurt by Eli, but without him being a tosser, we wouldn't have met."

"A tosser?"

I smiled at him. "You know, wanker."

He stepped in closer to me and pulled lightly on my beard. He smiled, but his eyes were serious. "I don't want to screw this up."

"Me either," I admitted. "And truth be told, Andrew, if one of us will fuck something up, it'll more than likely be me. I have relationship issues, remember?"

He kissed me softly. "Maybe all the more reason we should take things slower. If Sarah hadn't turned up, I'm pretty sure we'd be in bed right now."

I sighed and pulled him against me. "Agreed. Actually, I had us going at it like rabbits on the laundry floor."

He chuckled and pulled back a bit but kept his hands on my waist. "So, I think we should be clear though. By taking it slow, does that mean we wait for, you know, penetrative sex? Because while that's fine with me, I wouldn't be opposed to other things."

"Other things like what?"

His cheeks turned pink. "Like we did earlier."

"Blowjobs and handjobs? Because that's technically having sex."

His blush crept down his neck. "You know what I mean."

"Oh, you mean anal, butt-sex, fucking like rabbits."

He blanched at my crassness, and despite his raging blush, he nodded.

"Sorry. I shouldn't joke." I put my hands to his face. "This is the last time I'm going to mention his name. But just because Eli didn't want to have sex with you and just because

I'm agreeing to take things slow, doesn't mean you're not desirable. Because seriously, Andrew, you are incredibly sexy." He blushed scarlet. "And, like you, I want this to be something more than just physical. But I really have no clue how to gauge what's slow or not, so I'll take my cues from you. If you want to wait a day, a week, a month, a year, to fuck like rabbits on your laundry floor. I'll wait."

"A *year*?"

I laughed at the look of horror on his face. "Okay, let's just agree that a year is too long to wait."

He chuckled again. "I was thinking maybe a week or two... To be honest, I don't know if I'll be able to wait that long. I seem to have a permanent problem when you're around." He pressed his hips into mine to prove his point.

I could feel his *permanent problem*. It was rubbing against my *permanent problem* through our trousers. I laughed. Or groaned. Possibly both. "Me too."

He pressed his lips to mine, but before the kiss could get too serious, the washing machine beeped. He pulled away with a frustrated moan. "Saved by the bell," I mumbled, trying to laugh it off.

He shook his head adamantly. "Nope. I'll just throw your sheets in the dryer and put the next load in, then we're going to bed for handjobs or blowjobs and then you can nap."

And bossy Andrew was back. I had to admit, I liked bossy Andrew. He left the kitchen with a determined look on his face, and I followed. Only, he went down the hallway to the laundry, and I headed for the stairs. I figured he wouldn't have to wonder where I went if I left a trail of my clothes behind. My shirt fell on the bottom stair, I toed my shoes off at the top, my trousers near his bedroom door, and my undies near the bed.

By the time he'd followed my trail of breadcrumbs and

saw my underwear on the floor, he knew I was naked under the covers. "Which side do you prefer?" I asked.

His pupils were blown, his lips were parted, and his breaths were sharp. And there was a very prominent bulge in his pants. Without a word, he pulled his shirt off, then undid his pants, and slid them down his thighs to reveal his glorious cock. I flipped the covers back in silent invitation and he hesitated for a brief second.

"Don't worry about your sheets," I told him. "I promise I won't spill a drop."

He moaned gruffly and knelt on the bed. "It's not that," he said quietly. "I just like how you look in my bed."

I slid over and wrapped my hands around the backs of his thighs and took him into my mouth. And for the third time that day, we brought each other to climax.

Afterwards, when we were all wrapped up in each other's arms on what could possibly be the world's most comfortable bed, I napped like the dead.

FOUR

I woke up alone. It took me a second to realise I was in Andrew's room, but his side of the bed was empty. Disappointment slithered through me like a snake, but then I heard it.

He was playing his piano.

My clothes were in a half-folded pile at the end of the bed, and I smiled knowing he'd put them there for me. Such a simple, yet thoughtful gesture. It was ridiculous how happy that made me.

After getting dressed I used his bathroom, washed my hands then my face, squirted some toothpaste onto my finger, and did my best to clean up before going back downstairs. I didn't want to miss him playing.

He was still at his piano and he smiled as I walked over to lean against it. Without missing a beat, the song he was playing changed into something more funky and upbeat. It was some jazz number he knew by heart, and I couldn't help but smile as he played.

When that song was over, he took his hands from the keys. "Slept well?"

"Best nap ever," I told him. I nodded toward the piano keys. "Don't stop playing."

He gave me that eye-crinkling kind of smile and played a song that was more classical than jazz. Some grand concerto piece that I'm sure he played just to impress me. It worked. Though in all seriousness, he could play "Twinkle, Twinkle, Little Star" and I'd be impressed, but this was amazing.

This time when the song was over, the notes morphed into some random piece that was almost comical. And from the smile on his face, I wondered if it was from some cartoon I'd never seen, or if it was a musical extension of how happy he was in that moment. Because right then and there, standing in his living room, I knew there was no going back.

Not for me anyway.

I think he won a tiny piece of my heart that day. If he didn't have the whole damn thing before then, he certainly had part of it now.

I couldn't help myself. I strode over to him, took his face in my hands, and tilted his head back so I could kiss him. It made his fingers miss the keys, and he laughed into my mouth.

"You are something special, you know that?"

He hummed his answer. "Mmm, minty."

"I borrowed some toothpaste. Hope you don't mind." Before he could wonder if I was gross and used his toothbrush, I held up my finger. "I just kind of used my finger. Not great, but better than nothing."

"I can get you a toothbrush," he said. "I'm sure I have a pack of spares here."

I put my hand up in a stop. "Slow, remember? I think exchanging toothbrushes might be a little premature."

He frowned and nodded. "Okay, sure."

It was then that I noticed the light outside, or lack thereof.

"What time is it?" I asked, pulling out my phone. It was after six. "Jeez, I better get going home."

Andrew slowly stood up from his piano stool. "I'll drive you."

"I'm sure I can bus it."

"It's no problem. I need to grab some things from the store anyway. I'm a good boy and pack a lunch every day—I can't cook, but I can make a sandwich. I normally go in the morning, but my weekend was kind of thrown all out of whack."

I smiled at him. "In a bad way?"

"The very opposite of bad." He put his hand on my arm as he walked past. "I'll just grab your laundry." He came back out with everything washed and dried and neatly folded.

"What? You didn't iron them?"

He balked. "I'm not your maid."

I laughed and gave him a kiss on the cheek. "I'm just kidding. I'm very grateful that you even offered for me to do this here."

He sighed deeply. "You're welcome."

"Oh, before I forget, where's your phone?"

He cautiously pulled it from his pocket. "Here, why?"

"We need to add another photo to your Facebook."

"Oh." His cheeks tinted with that delicious pink. "Right."

"Is that okay?"

"Sure."

I took his phone and pressed the camera icon, and putting my arm around him and nuzzling my nose into his cheek, we posed for a selfie. After we'd taken a few, he selected the best —and by that, I mean the one he thought he looked best in— and he uploaded it onto his timeline. "Um, should I—" He stopped. "Oh, don't worry."

I hated when people said that. Of course it made me worry. "Should you what?"

"Oh, I was just wondering..." He shook his head. "You know how people change their relationship status... It's silly, don't worry."

"It's not silly."

"I'm just excited about this," he said, looking at his phone instead of me, though I could see a blush creep down his neck. "But I'm supposed to take it slow, and maybe telling the world about us is being too forward. Sarah was right. I do rush into things. I've jumped without looking into every relationship I've ever had. Posting photos is one thing; announcing it is a bit different."

"Andrew," I said quietly. I waited for him to look at me before continuing. "If you want to post it, then post it. Tell the world you scored the hottest boyfriend ever. Although they'll know that from the photo."

He laughed and looked back down at his phone. "I won't. Not yet. I don't want to jinx anything. Though I'll have to tell people at work tomorrow. Well, Michelle will know straight away. She's kind of like what Lola is to you. She'll see it on my face before I can say a word anyway, and she will have commented on this photo within the hour. She's going to want to know every detail."

I groaned, and his eyes flashed to mine. "You just reminded me. Lola is no doubt still at the shop, waiting for me to get back. It'll be midnight before she stops interrogating me."

"What will you tell her?" he asked. There was a vulnerability in his eyes that I didn't like to see.

"That we're taking it slow, but the term *officially dating* was used."

Andrew smiled at that. "Sounds good to me."

"So, what's our plans for this week?" I asked. "I mean, do we make plans? Is that what boyfriends do?" It sounded weird for me to even say that. "Is that what officially dating even means? I have no idea."

"I'm pretty sure boyfriends make plans," he said with a slow nod, fighting a smile. "And yes, I think that's what officially dating means."

"Dinner Tuesday?" I asked. "I'll cook."

"You cook?"

I feigned offence. "Can I cook? I'll have you know, I make the best spag bol ever. It's not glamorous but it's good."

"Spag bol?"

"Spaghetti Bolognese."

"Is that an Australian thing?"

"Yep. We shorten everything. Don't worry, you'll get used to it."

He smiled at that. "I'm looking forward to that."

I kissed him softly and left my lips pressed to his for a few beats of my heart. "Thank you for today. And thank you for coming after me last night. Thank you for telling whatshisname to get lost, and thank you for breakfast. Thank you for smelling unbelievably good all the time, and thank you for playing your piano for me."

Andrew laughed but put his hand to my face, closed his eyes, and kissed me. He left his forehead pressed to mine and breathed in deep. "You're very welcome." He pulled away and said, "I better get you home or there'll be no taking it slow, and I'm not sure I can come four times in one day."

I laughed and smiled all the way home.

Until I walked through the shop door and Lola dragged me, literally, from the front door to the back cubicle, shooting questions at me like a machine gun. Oh who am I kidding? I was still smiling then too.

FIVE

"He wants to take it slow?" Lola asked. "I don't know if that makes him sweet or crazy."

"He says that's what he does," I explained. "He gets ahead of himself and gets carried away, and it ends up a fizzled out mess. He doesn't want to do that with me."

"See? That's what makes him sweet," Lola said.

"And that includes holding off on sex for a while."

"And that's what makes him crazy."

I laughed. "He's not perfect."

"Much."

I found myself smirking. "Much."

"Well, I am so happy you're taking a chance on him," Lola said. She squeezed my hand. "You deserve to be happy."

"Thanks," I mumbled, embarrassed. "He's kind of amazing."

Lola bounced and squeed. "Oh, look at you! You're a smitten kitten."

Smitten kitten? I swear a piece of my manliness just died. "Promise me you won't ever say those words again."

She just smiled and hummed dreamily. "And I take it he's perfectly fine with you meeting a new client tomorrow?"

Oh. "Um, I don't think he knows."

Lola stared at me. "He'll be okay with it, won't he?"

"He should be," I said. "He knows what I do for a job. Nothing has changed overnight there."

She nodded, seemingly appeased, then started on a new subject. "So, you're cooking him dinner on Tuesday night?"

And so our conversation went on until Gabe had had enough—or maybe he took pity on me—and dragged her home. I went upstairs, remade my bed, and found myself staring at my phone.

Should I text him? Is that what boyfriends do? Is that crossing the taking-it-slow boundaries?

So, ignoring my phone, I ate some dinner instead and then I got to thinking... why hadn't he texted me?

I put my phone on the kitchen counter and stared at it like it had knocked my world off kilter.

Which it kind of had. Well, not my phone exactly, but since when did I worry about shit like this? What had it been? A fucking day?

I snatched up my phone and went to Messages and found his name.

> Is me texting you right now taking it slow?
> Because I'm starting to overthink this shit
> and don't want to get it wrong but if I want
> to text you, I can, right?

I hit send, before I could overthink that, and threw my phone back on the counter. I was grabbing a drink from the fridge when my phone buzzed, and I almost busted a valve in my heart trying to see if it was him that replied.

It was.

> Texting me is fine. More than fine, actually. And jsyk, that photo I posted on Facebook has garnered a lot of comments.

I smiled like a school kid with a crush, then of course looked around my flat to see if anyone saw how ridiculous I was being, then shook my head at myself because I lived alone. Of course no one saw me. I took my phone and bottle of water to the couch and collapsed onto it, still smiling at the small screen in my hand.

I quickly replied.

> Garnered? Did you really just use the word garnered?

His reply was immediate.

> Shut up.

I laughed out loud.

> So, the comments that have been garnered, are they favourable?

I was expecting a quick response, but instead the phone rang in my hand. It was Andrew. "Are you giving me crap?"

I laughed again. "Absolutely. In Australia, we would call that 'taking the piss.' Did you really tell me to shut up?"

"Yes I did." He breathed in deep. "I'm glad you texted me."

"I wasn't going to," I admitted. "Then I struggled with what the criteria for taking things slow was and wondered if texting you after we'd spent the last two days together was crossing some line in the handbook of boyfriend etiquette, and then I realised how idiotic I was being and thought *fuck it*. Hence the text."

"Hence. And you—How did you put it?—'took the piss' out of me for saying garnered."

"Shut up."

He laughed into the phone, and the sound sent a rush of warmth through my chest.

"Lola gave me an inquisition the Spanish would be proud of," I told him.

He chuckled again. "Yes, Sarah called me not too long ago. And my mother. Apparently showing the world via social media that I was being cosy with a new beau—those were her words, not mine—but I hadn't told her yet, has earned me a lunch date where said Spanish Inquisition will no doubt take place."

Now it was me who laughed. "Sounds like fun."

"Yes, fun like a Black Knight flesh wound."

"Did you just quote Monty Python?"

"Did you just get my Monty Python reference?"

I snorted. "*The Holy Grail* is one of my favourites."

I swear I could hear him smiling. "Mine too."

Then his doorbell sounded in the background. "Expecting someone?" I asked.

"Yep. Dinner. I told you I don't cook."

"So, what's on tonight's menu?"

"Mexican. Bean salad with a side of burrito."

God, he made me laugh. "Okay, I'll let you go. Have fun. I'll text you tomorrow night."

"Okay. Bye."

After I disconnected the call, I smiled at my phone like a simpleton until I went to bed. Though I kinda worried about not telling him about my appointment with a new client tomorrow. It's not something I ever had to worry about before, but now that Lola mentioned it, I couldn't help but wonder what Andrew would think. I took my phone off the bedside table and considered shooting him a quick text, reminding him I was starting a new job tomorrow.

And then I chickened out, because what if he *did* have an issue with it? And then I told myself to man the fuck up and tell him. Just as I was about to do it, my phone buzzed in my hand with a message.

It was Andrew.

> Jsyk, any doubts of my ability to come four times in one day were unfounded.

I groaned at the mental images of him jerking himself off in bed. Or in the shower. Or onto my stomach, or in my mouth... Now my balls were aching with need.

> That is so not fair.

His response took a little while.

> You're welcome.

Needless to say, that was a contest I just couldn't let him win.

I WAS EARLY TO MY APPOINTMENT TO MEET MY NEW client. I preferred to give them the impression that I was cool, calm, and collected about it, because more often than not, they were stressed and heartbroken and needed someone who was in control.

Lance was different. Recommended to my services from one of his friends, who was an old client of mine, Gerard, a guy I didn't particularly like. He was the tosser who thought he could buy anything and anyone he wanted, and I knew before Lance had even said a word, he was just like his friend.

The meeting place was a coffee house on Wiltshire, the hub of downtown LA. It wasn't his expensive suit or his Italian leather loafers, not even his slicked back hair or smarmy smile that gave him away as being a tosser. It was in his eyes. They were dark, almost black, not that that was a bad thing—I'd seen some gorgeous smouldering dark eyes— but these were flat. Like a shark's eyes. There was something about him that pinged my arsehole-o-meter, but willing to give him the benefit of the doubt, I stood up, shook his hand, and introduced myself.

"Thanks for meeting me," he said. He waved his hand and clicked his fingers at the wait staff like they were his personal servants without so much as a sideways glance or smile. Yep, arsehole-o-meter officially pinged.

But he was the paying client, so I sipped my green tea and smiled. "So, Gerard recommended me." It wasn't a question.

"Yes. And you're as good looking as he said. I think you'll work just fine." The waiter arrived at our table, and Lance barked an order at him. I thanked the waiter because Lance clearly thought it was beneath him to show some fucking manners.

I gave Lance a tight smile and cut right to the chase. "So, there's someone you want back in your life?"

"Yes."

"Male or female?"

"Male." His eyes narrowed. "Is that an issue?"

I presumed his friend Gerard had told him I was gay. I'd worked with him and his ex-boyfriend after all. *Was Lance testing me?* I looked him right in the eye. "Certainly not. Payment terms are half up front, half at the conclusion of the job. I can't stress enough that the final result may or may not be what you want. I can't guarantee his response. What I can guarantee you is an answer and the truth. It's not my job to convince him to come back to you. It's my job to make him jealous, and hopefully, he'll realise he made a mistake and wants you back. Terms are full payment, regardless of outcome."

The waiter put Lance's coffee on the table, and again Lance didn't even acknowledge the poor guy. Seriously, a fucking smile or nod didn't cost a cent. Instead, he smiled at me. "Sounds reasonable. But I don't think what I have in mind is your usual MO."

I kept my expression neutral. "And why's that?"

"I don't want us to pretend to be together. I want you to befriend him."

"And why would I want to do that?"

"I have no problem in finding some hot little piece of arse to grope in a bar if I wanted to make him jealous." He took a self-righteous breath. "That's not what I need. I need you to befriend him and gain his trust."

Okay, this was getting bizarre. "Why?"

"He won't see me."

For good reason, I thought. "Then I think our meeting is redundant, Mr Nader. If the client refuses to see you or even speak to you, then I can't help you." I stood up, officially ending this meeting.

He put his hand on my arm. "It's not like that. It's his family. They're a large Greek family and very strict. When they found out he was seeing me..." He shook his head, and for the first time since I'd met him, he showed some kind of emotion. I sat back down to hear him out. He spoke in a whisper. "When he came to tell me we were finished, he had bruises." He put his hand to his own cheekbone. "I begged him to tell me who had hurt him, but he wouldn't say. He just left."

Oh, shit. "If he's in some kind of trouble, you should have called the police. Not me."

"He would only deny it if they questioned him," Lance said quickly. "It's his father who he's afraid of. I'm sure of it. That's why I need you to befriend him. Talk to him."

I studied him for a long moment, gauging his sincerity. His reaction seemed genuine and honest, not that I knew him at all. "Then what?"

"I want to see him, I won't deny it." He swallowed hard. "I love him."

"How long ago did he leave?"

"Three weeks ago."

"And you've not spoken to him since?"

He shook his head.

"How old is he?"

"Twenty-one."

Lance would have easily been thirty, maybe thirty-two or three. "Where did you meet?"

"At The Standard. I know he's younger than me, but what we had was... special. We just clicked from the first day. You know what that's like?"

Funnily enough, now I did. "How long were you together?"

"A year."

"His name?"

"Yanni Tomaras."

"Where does he work?"

"He was attending LA Actors Academy. It's a college in West Hollywood, but I think he's quit or is taking some time off, at least. He used to work at a café near the campus, but he hasn't been in for a shift since he left me."

"You've tried to track him down?"

"Only at school and work," he admitted. "Where his family wouldn't find out."

"What makes you think I will be even able to find him? I'm not a private eye. I don't typically find missing people."

"Gerard said you were very good. And Yanni's not missing, he's just gone quiet because his family are homophobes. God only knows what they threatened him with. I don't want to involve the police, and God, private detectives are worse than real cops. It could put him in an even worse position than he is now if they go sticking their noses into his family, know what I mean?"

I took a deep breath and weighed up my options. Sure, Lance was a wanker, but if this kid was in some trouble, then maybe I should help. Or, at the very least, maybe if I could track him down and assess the whole crazy situation for myself, then I could decide what to do. And that was *if* I could find him.

I reached into my jacket pocket and pulled out my small notepad and handed it to him. "Write down his name, date of birth, the college he went to, classes he took, the café he worked at, places he hung out, names of friends. Anything you can think of. I'll also need your email address and other contact details."

He scribbled furiously, and when he gave it back to me, I said, "No promises. I don't even know if I'll be able to find him."

Lance smiled. "I have every faith."

I RELAYED MY MEETING TO LOLA AND EMILIO. EMILIO agreed that something sounded off about the whole thing, and Lola cautioned me to follow my gut. "I know, I know," I agreed. "Lance Nader is a tosser, but what if this ex-boyfriend needs some help? It can't hurt to look into it."

"So, if you met this Tosser-Guy in a bar…?" Lola trailed off suggestively.

"I'd run a mile," I said without hesitating. "He pinged my arsehole-o-meter before he even sat down."

Lola made that face that told me I was being an idiot. "You're saying all the things I'd expect you to say if you turned the job down," she said.

"I know." I sighed loudly. "I might not even be able to find the guy."

She rubbed my arm. "I trust your judgement, Spence. If something doesn't feel right, just tell Tosser-guy it's no bueno."

I finally gave her a smile. "I will."

"You look good today," she said, dropping the subject of my new client, who had not-so-subtly been given the nickname of Tosser-Guy. Because that's what he was.

I looked down at my shirt and pants. I'd worn this before. "Um, thanks?"

She laughed. "It's not your clothes. It's you. Look at you being all happy and shit."

"Oh." I knew what she was referring to. She was about to tell me I had some inner glow from love or sex or something equally embarrassing. "I like your dress. Is that new?"

She wasn't fooled. "Nice try."

"I'm serious. Is that sunshine yellow?"

She narrowed her eyes at me but went back to unpacking a box of new jewellery for Daniela. "Are those new Prince Albert designs?"

"Yep. Want one?"

My dick shrank back inside my body at the thought. "Ah, no thanks."

She laughed. "Andrew might like it."

I ignored her. "The yellow of your dress really suits your pink hair," I added. "Same tone. And the thin black belt and matching black high heels is a great combination."

Lola laughed and shook her head at me. "You're not deflecting anything with me, Spencer Cohen. Don't think I don't know what you're trying to do."

"I'm not trying to do anything," I lied.

She tugged on my beard. "I'm happy for you and Andrew. Even if you don't want to talk about it."

I laughed incredulously. "I have talked about it. I've told you as much as I can about me and Andrew without divulging our favourite lube."

Someone laughed outside the cubicle.

"On that note," I said, walking to the cubicle curtain. I spoke to whoever the hell was listening. "I will see you good people tomorrow." I stuck my head out to see Emilio. "Need anything, man?"

He looked up from where he was inking a customer. "Nah."

"Dinner later?"

"No hot date tonight?"

I groaned. "No."

"That's tomorrow night," Lola yelled out from her cubicle.

I took a deep breath, but it did little to stem the traitorous blush that heated my stupid cheeks.

Emilio laughed. "Nah, I'm finishing up early tonight. Shop'll be shut by seven."

"Okay. Call me if you need anything. And tell Daniela I said thank you for yesterday. And the night before for helping me with my Academy Award winning Maker's Mark performance." I cringed as the memory of bourbon burned in my throat. "Any night this week you guys want dinner, it's on me."

Emilio grinned at me. "Any night, but not tomorrow night."

"Well no, tomorrow night is... yeah whatever, just not tomorrow night."

He laughed. "I'll tell my beautiful woman," he said. "She'll take you up on that offer, my friend."

"Good. We'll aim for Friday night dinner, if something doesn't change in the meantime," I said happily. I stopped at the cubicle on my way to the back door. "And Lola, you and Gabe included. It's my treat."

"Will Andrew be joining us?" she asked. Her tone was a mix of both teasing and hopeful.

"I don't know," I said quietly. "I'll ask."

Her smile was beautiful. "Okay!"

I withheld a groan, but I was back to smiling. I had to wonder if I'd ever stopped.

I SPENT THE AFTERNOON DOING ONLINE SEARCHES for Yanni Tomaras. He had no social media accounts, well, not under his real name. Not that I could find, anyway. By cross-referencing locations and photos, even likes and anything that had been favourited, there was no other Yanni that was remotely close to the pictures Lance had sent me.

I tried a varied combination of his name, date of birth, and address. Then I added in his college and class information, coupled with his place of employment, and surprisingly, I made some headway.

I must have lost track of time because the next thing I knew, my phone rang. Andrew's name flashed up on screen.

"Hey," I answered.

"Hi."

I was one hundred percent certain I was doing that ridiculous smiling thing, just from the sound of his voice. "How was your day?"

"Good," he replied. "I survived the colleague inquisition, though only barely."

"Was it rough?"

He groaned. "Painful."

I chuckled. "Yes, Lola accosted me again today. Though my diversion tactics of complimenting her outfit were countered, and it's true what they say, resistance is futile."

He made a happy sound. "Well, I'm having lunch with my mom tomorrow."

"Remember," I said seriously. "When in doubt, compliment her outfit."

"You just said that didn't work."

"Well, it didn't work on Lola, but she knows all my cunning plans."

"Did you just quote *Blackadder*?"

"Do you know *Blackadder*?"

"Well, obviously."

I laughed. "My Aunt Marvie loved all the British shows."

"My dad was born in England," Andrew said. "Came here when he was very young, but his family loves them too. We grew up watching the BBC."

"I didn't know that," I mused. "That you're half English."

"Where do you think I get my awesome tan from?"

God, he made me laugh. "Well, for what it's worth, I hear pale is the new tan. All the rage in LA at the moment. I saw an article in *Pasty Living*."

"You're not funny," he said, though I could hear the smile in his voice. "And I'm not pasty."

"No, you've got great skin, I must say. When you get here tomorrow night for dinner, you might have to get naked just so I can be sure though."

"Is that right?"

"Yep. Absolutely."

He sighed. "I'm sure I can arrange something. I'd hate to disappoint you."

It was quiet where he was. There was no background noise. "Are you home already?"

"Yep. Been home for a while."

I checked my watch. Shit, it was six-thirty. "I didn't realise the time."

"What did you get up to today?"

"I met a new client today."

Silence.

"Oh."

"Yeah," I added quickly, defensively. "He's a bit of a wanker, and it's all a bit weird, to be honest."

More silence.

"Andrew?"

"Yeah, I'm here. I just... why didn't you tell me?"

"I did. Just now. I just told you."

"No, I mean, before. Why didn't you tell me before?"

"I forgot about it, to be honest. I had a life changing weekend, as you might recall. And I was going to tell you last night, but then you sent me a text about coming four times and my stupid brain went on a one-way trip to pornville. There was no coming back from that... Well, there was coming... I had to see whether I could manage four times in one day—well, since I was seventeen anyway—and I couldn't let you beat me. I'm competitive like that."

He was silent again, but then he laughed. "What?"

"Do you want me to repeat all of that?"

"You didn't message me back to say that you did a fourth."

"I was in an orgasm coma, thanks to you. I wasn't capable of texting."

He laughed, but he was serious when he asked, "And your weekend was life-changing?"

"Yes. I seemed to have scored myself a smokin' hot boyfriend. And that's a first for me. A boyfriend of any kind, that is." I sighed and spoke quietly, "So forgive me if I forget to tell you things... It's just that I've never let anyone in. Ever."

I could hear him suck back a breath. After a beat of silence, his voice was soft when he asked, "Smoking hot, huh?"

"Yeah, totally. He was on the cover of *Pasty Living* and everything."

Now he laughed again. "I'm sorry. I just tend to get on the defensive."

"That's okay. I tend to get on the clueless. So we're even."

He let out a long breath. "So, a new fake boyfriend, huh?"

"If you mean new client, then yes. But I'm not pretending anything with this guy."

"What do you mean?"

I just realised how that must have sounded. "No, no, no. I mean, I don't have to pretend to be with him or anything like that. I don't have to get to know him, or touch him, or even hang out with him."

"Oh."

"Would it bother you if I did?" I asked. I knew the answer to that already. It clearly did bother him. "It's normally what I do. It's how I met you! So you knew what I did for a job, Andrew."

"I know," he replied quietly. "And I'm trying not to have an issue with it, but the idea of you spending time with another guy, the way we did…"

"Yeah, but I don't spend time with them like we did. I don't normally do half of what we did with any other client. I told you, you were different. From day one, things were different with you."

"I know," he said again. "I'm allowed to feel a little jealous. I mean, would you prefer me to not tell you how something makes me feel?"

"No, I don't want you to censor anything."

"I know it's your job, Spencer, and I don't have an issue with what you do. I just… will you have to kiss him?"

"No, I won't. It's a weird case. He doesn't want me to pretend to be his boyfriend. But I can't promise that another case down the track won't require me to hold some guy's hand, or dance with him in a bar or something like that."

Again with the silence, but this needed saying. I shouldn't change what I did for a living just because I had a boyfriend. Should I?

"Can I ask you something?" His voice was kinda quiet.

"Sure."

"If I had to, as part of my job, go out this weekend to a bar and kiss some guy to secure a deal with a production company, would that bother you?"

I pictured him, all smiles at another guy and kissing him, pretend or not, and my stomach twisted. Would it bother me?

Yes. Yes, yes, yes. Hell yes, it would.

"No."

He laughed. "You can't lie."

"Okay, it totally would. The thought of another guy kissing you bothers me." I groaned and dug the heel of my left hand into my eye. "I have a vivid imagination, and you'd be wearing your blue and red Argyle sweater and have those little lines at your eyes when you laugh, and then you'd look at him, then he'd put his hands on you and lean in... And yes, it bothers me."

"That was pretty detailed."

"Like I said, I have a very healthy imagination."

He laughed. "So I don't have a problem with it because it's your job. I know that. I knew it before I agreed to give this relationship a shot. But yes, it bothers me that some other guy gets to touch you. Even if it means nothing. I would never ask you to stop doing what you do, Spencer. Please tell me you understand that."

"Sure." The thought never crossed my mind to actually quit doing what I do. Financially, I didn't even have to do it, but I enjoyed the people aspect of it. I loved the personal nature of the whole set up, and I loved helping people get their lives back on track.

"But it just means that if you ever do have to take some guy out on a fake date, you better make it up to me."

Finally, I smiled. "Now, that I can do."

"Should I be more specific?"

"Please do."

"Well, I'm not opposed to fancy dinners."

"Really? Food? You can make me do any one thing, and it's take you out for dinner?"

"What's wrong with that?"

"I was expecting something a little dirtier, to be honest. Like naked, full-body massages, or the most mind-blowing rim-job you've ever had."

"Spencer!"

I laughed. "What? Believe me, if you're gonna put in demands for me to make it up to you, that's the kind of stuff you need to say."

He scoffed. "Rim-jobs? Jesus, you can't..."

"Can't what?"

"You can't just say stuff like that."

"You're blushing right now, aren't you?"

"Not telling."

"You so are," I said with a laugh. "Which tells me one of two things. One, you happen to really like rim-jobs, or two, you've never had one. You've always wanted to know what it feels like, but you've been too afraid to ask."

"Veto."

I burst out laughing. "No calling veto! That rule has been taken off the table. Not that it matters, because your vetoing tells me it's definitely the second one. You've never experienced another man's mouth on your arse."

I could hear him swallow.

"And you want to. And Andrew?"

He cleared his throat. "Yeah?"

"I'm only too happy to oblige."

He let out a nervous laugh. "How did this conversation end up in the gutter so quickly?"

"We're two men who are trying to abstain from fucking each other's brains out. It's going to be the topic of conversation until it happens," I told him. "Probably worse after it does."

He groaned into the phone. "You're killing me here."

"If you tell me you need to end the call so you can wank, I'll be very disappointed."

He laughed but it was a pained sound. "What if I said it was because dinner just arrived?"

"I'd call bullshit. And still be disappointed you didn't let me listen."

His breathing was heavy in my ear. "Um, do you think

tomorrow night when I come over for dinner we could possibly put an end to our suffering?"

"Nope. It's too soon." And this was too much fun. "But just so you know, I'm going to rim you."

His breath hitched and then I heard it. A zipper.

"Did you just unzip yourself?" I asked quietly. "Have you got your hand on your gorgeous cock already?"

"Um..."

I smiled. He totally did. "Good. Fuck your fist like you want to fuck my arse."

"Oh, Spencer," he whispered. I could hear the faint slick noise of his hand pumping his cock. The mental image of that sent a surge of precum to the tip of my dick. I slid my hand underneath the waistband of my trousers, and yeah, I was wet at the tip of my dick. I gave myself a quick few pumps, imagining him doing the same.

"And tomorrow night, I'm going to fuck your arse with my tongue."

He let out a strangled cry as he came. He was obviously trying to be quiet but couldn't seem to hold it in. "Oh, God."

"Mmmm," I groaned, knowing my words had brought him undone. "You're so fucking hot."

His breaths were ragged, and he laughed. "I can't believe I just did that." Then, before he could be any more embarrassed, his doorbell rang. "Shit! That's dinner. I'm not even kidding. I have to go."

I was still laughing when the call ended abruptly in my ear. But I was also still hard. I considered going into the shower but thought *fuck it*. I undid my pants, pulled them down around my hips, and remembering the sounds of Andrew coming so close in my ear, I brought myself to climax.

About two minutes later, I was still lazy-smiling at my

lounge room wall when my phone buzzed with a message.

> The Chinese food delivery guy thinks I'm weird. I blame you.

I laughed.

> You're welcome. And Chinese food on a Monday night, seriously?

> Shut up. Its wanton soup and steamed vegetables. But this is the reason I work out so much.

> I will teach you how to cook.

> Will you be naked?

> Yes.

> Even better.

I smiled ridiculously at my phone as I replied,

> Oh, btw, you totally just made me come.

> Talking about cooking naked can make you come?

> No, listening to your phone sex sounds totally made me come.

> Oh.

> Are you blushing?

> Veto.

SIX

THE NEXT MORNING, I WENT THROUGH LANCE'S emails again and took down all the details on paper to get a clearer picture in my head. The school Yanni went to was on Melrose, as was the café he worked at. So I started there. I called, and after a few rings, a girl answered above the clatter and noise of a coffee shop. "Hi," I started cheerfully. "Wow, you sound really busy. I don't mean to keep you, but I was wondering if you could tell me if Yanni will be in today?"

"Um," she stalled. "Hang on one sec."

The sound muffled, like she put her hand over the mouthpiece. Then a man spoke. "Who is this?"

"My name is Spencer," I told him. "I have classes with Yanni, and I haven't seen him. I thought maybe he was still working there?"

"He doesn't work here anymore," he replied.

"Oh. Well, do you know where I might be able to find him?" I pushed.

"I can't help you," he said bluntly and disconnected the call.

Right, then. Next effort was the college. Which of course

was a dead end. The woman I spoke to was like a brick wall. "I wouldn't give out student personal information even if it wasn't against the law," she said, before telling me not to call back. Honestly, I expected nothing less, but I had to try anyway.

I closed down my laptop, pocketed my phone, and went downstairs to help Emilio out in the tattoo shop instead. I actually liked getting in and doing the mundane stuff that Emilio didn't really have time for. I took a delivery of sterile equipment and restacked the boxes in the cabinets, did a quick stock audit, put in an order for more ink, answered the phone, took bookings, double-checked timeslots, and helped Daniela when she needed a second pair of hands. I fit in there, I belonged. Wearing a T-shirt so my tattooed arms were exposed, people who came in didn't look twice at me. In fact, I'd come to know most of Emilio's regulars by name and would chat with them while they spent hours in the chair getting inked or pierced or whatever. Sometimes they just came in to say hi.

And it helped to keep my mind off my newest case. Well, I thought it did. "Everything okay, Spencer?" Emilio asked. "You keep cleaning that glass counter top, you'll wear it out."

I hadn't really even realised I was still rubbing it. I looked at the paper towel in my hand to find it worn through. "Oh, yeah. Just this new client," I said.

"It's bugging you too much," Emilio said. "You need to tell the client you can't help him."

I nodded. "Yeah. I know."

Lola came through from the back. Her pink hair was styled in 1950s victory rolls, which matched the rockabilly style black dress and her pink high heels matched her hair. I'd never not seen her look a million dollars. I hadn't even noticed she was here, a sure sign of just how distracted I'd been. I relayed my findings, or lack thereof, on the guy called Yanni.

"I'm heading downtown tomorrow," Lola said. "I could drop you off at the college if you want?"

"It can't hurt, I guess," I said. "Thanks, that'd be good."

Lola eyed me cautiously. "Sure it's not something else bothering you?"

"Like what?"

"Andrew."

"What about him?"

She smiled. "Was he okay with it?"

"Yeah. In the beginning he was concerned, but in the end he was fine. I think he just kind of forgot what it is I do." I shrugged. "I'm seeing him tonight, so we'll talk about it more then, I guess."

"Ooh, any plans?"

"I'm cooking him dinner," I said proudly. "I'm going to attempt to teach him how to make spaghetti bolognaise. Nothing too fancy, but considering he can't make toast, I thought it was best to start with the basics. Which reminds me"—I looked at my watch—"I better go to the store. Anybody need anything?"

"Nope," Lola answered. "Not me. I'm heading off soon myself, but I'll pick you up out front tomorrow at eight."

I kissed her cheek. "You are the light of my life."

She fluttered her eyelashes and posed like a fair-maiden. "Why thank you, but I've seen the way you look at another, and I think I've been rendered to second place."

I put my hand to my heart and faked a gasp. "Never! My heart is yours and yours alone."

Lola put the back of her hand to her forehead and played along. "Alas, if only we were born to another time."

I bowed in front of her. "If only your heart didn't belong to another."

Lola curtsied. "If I only had a penis."

Everyone laughed. Even Emilio had to stop tattooing; not only was he laughing, but the guy getting tattooed laughed as well. Lola and I were always joking around with each other like that.

I kissed Lola's knuckles, like a true gentleman, before walking to the door. I called out, "Last call for anything at the grocery store."

No one wanted anything so I walked out, still with a smile on my face. I tried not to think about how good life was right now. I didn't want to jinx it. But I couldn't remember ever feeling this happy. Not for a lot of years, anyway. I also tried not to read too much into my relationship with Andrew. Sure, he was great and made me happy, but my entire happiness wasn't hinged on him. I wouldn't allow it to be. Because, if for whatever reason he decided I wasn't right for him, then I wouldn't allow my world to fall apart.

I couldn't let that happen again.

I guessed it was part of the defence mechanism I'd learned to put up around my heart. And I couldn't deny it. If Andrew did decide I wasn't the one for him, then I'd be devastated. I knew it was only early days, but he was a remarkable guy. He knew my family history and was still interested in getting to know me, in spending time with me. And that made me incredibly happy. But I could compartmentalise enough to know that the fact I was letting someone past my defensive walls was a huge thing for me.

It showed me I was ready, finally after all these years, to move on with my life.

I wasn't worthless, like my father had told me. I wasn't unlovable, like he'd implied.

And so even if Andrew and I didn't work out, I'd made incredible groundwork that my old psychiatrist would have been proud of. I'm sure she'd have told me exactly what Lola had said. I deserved to be happy. And I was happy. My life here in LA was great. I had the best friends, who doubled as my family, and Andrew was just the icing on the cake.

Mmm, cake. I wondered what kind of cake was his favourite. Did he even like cake? It was something I'd never thought to ask... When I arrived at the store, I headed straight for the bakery section and pulled out my phone. I shot him a quick text.

> Do you like cake?

His response took a minute.

> Is that a euphemism?

I laughed at the screen, not caring what the people standing next to me thought.

> LOL No. Actual cake. Chocolate, caramel, vanilla?

> Um, cake with fruit?

I squinted at his reply.

> What? Nobody likes fruit in their cake. Except old people. At Christmastime. It's like a crime against humanity.

My phone rang almost immediately. Of course it was him. There was no hello or anything. "Crime against humanity?"

"Yes. No cake should have fruit in it. It's an insult to the cake part."

He laughed. "Where are you?"

"In the cake aisle at the shop."

"At the shop?"

"Grocery store. Seriously, American people need to learn Australian. And they don't even have fruity cakes for sale when it's not December."

"Yes, they do."

"No, there was a petition. All the real cakes, like chocolate and buttercream, decided that fruitcake didn't qualify as a cake."

I could hear the smile in his voice. "No?"

"Nope. It was decided that fruitcake contained more fruit than cake, therefore it was not eligible."

"Really?"

"Yep, really. But then it didn't technically fit into the fruit section either. And the alcohol section certainly didn't want it."

"Is this conversation going somewhere?"

"Yes. It's going back to the chocolate cake section."

Andrew laughed. "Chocolate cake it is, then."

"Do you even like cake?"

"Um, not really."

I stopped walking. "But you said you did."

"Well, I thought I had to pick one. Like it was a trivia question or, well, I don't even know."

"Dear God. You'd pick *fruitcake*?"

He laughed again. "If I were to pick dessert, it wouldn't be cake at all. I would choose ice cream. Gelato, actually."

I turned toward the dairy section. "Now, gelato I can certainly do. What flavour's your favourite?"

"Is there a right and wrong answer?"

I chuckled into the phone. "Yes. But I'm not telling."

"Well then, I would choose lemon gelato."

I stopped walking again. "Seriously? What is it with you and fruit?"

He was still smiling, I could tell. "If you've never had lemon gelato, you are surely missing out."

"Do I need to try it?"

"Absolutely."

"All right. But if it's gross, you owe me chocolate cake."

He laughed. "Deal."

"And the good stuff. I like mud cake with the ganache. Not some supermarket bought one."

"You were going to get me a store-bought one."

"Well, true. But that was before. Anyway, if you don't cook at home, it's not like you'd go to a store anyway."

"I go to the store," he said defensively. "Just not for... food that requires cooking."

I laughed. "Well, you're cooking tonight."

He groaned. "Really?"

"Yep. What time will you finish work?"

"I'll get to your place around seven. Is that okay?"

I looked at my watch. It was almost five. "That's fine."

"I was hoping you were joking about the cooking thing. I thought..."

"You thought what?"

He cleared his throat. "Oh, never mind. I have to go. I'll see you tonight."

The phone offered only silence in my ear. I figured he must have had a co-worker walk in, so I finished my shopping, lemon gelato included, and went home.

At five minutes to seven there was a knock at my door. With the jazz funk album he chose for me playing softly in the background, I opened the door to find Andrew standing there, all fucking gorgeous and smiling. It had been, what? Not even two days since I'd seen him? And he was somehow even better looking than I remembered. I wanted to grab his knitted vest and drag him inside so I could kiss him, but instead, because I had manners, I stepped aside. "Please, come in."

He walked in and shoved his hands in his pockets like he was nervous. "You're playing the album I got you."

"I am." I closed the door behind him and stepped right in up close, so our lips were almost touching. He smelled fresh-showered and delicious, and I breathed his scent in. "Hello," I whispered.

He kissed me, and I had to stop myself from pushing him back against the door and kissing him until he couldn't stand up. I wanted to. God, I wanted to. I pulled my mouth from his, all ragged-breaths and swollen lips, and could offer no more than a one-word sentence. "Dinner."

Andrew frowned, or possibly pouted. He looked right at my mouth and licked his lips. "We could order in. I'll pay."

I laughed and took a step back from him. He was so damn intoxicating. "Tempting. Really fucking tempting, but no. I promised I'd show you how to cook."

He looked into the kitchen. "You weren't kidding, were you?"

I shook my head. "No. Why did you think I was joking?"

He blushed from his cheeks right down underneath his collar. It was then I noticed he had showered before he came over. I remembered back to our conversation about dinner tonight and how it evolved into a conversation about rimming...

"Did you think dinner was a euphemism for something else?" I asked.

His eyes flashed to mine, and his voice squeaked. "Um. Maybe?"

"As in dinner would be *eating* something else? Like arse."

He barked out a laugh. "Don't just say it like that!"

I grabbed his hand and led him into the kitchen, or more precisely to stand in front of a chopping board that had all the ingredients for tonight's dinner on it. He looked down at it like it was a Chinese trigonometry equation, and trying not to laugh, I stood behind him. I put my hands on his hips and my lips at the back of his ear. "First we eat dinner, then I eat you. Deal?"

"You can't just say stuff like that to me," he said gruffly. He half turned his head so his cheek was touching my nose. "Or we won't be cooking dinner."

God give me strength. He was killing me. I playfully gnashed my teeth at his neck. "Later. I promise. Now, pick up the knife, Andrew," I urged him. "We need the onion to be finely chopped."

He hesitated to pick up the onion. "Um."

"Have you ever cut an onion before?"

"Why would I want to do that?"

I laughed into his shoulder. "Okay, so hold the onion down on the chopping board and slice the top and bottom off," I instructed. I put my hands over his, so while he held the knife, I guided his hand, and together we peeled and sliced the onion. He only complained about the smell and burning eyes about twenty times. Then we did the garlic and the tomatoes, and I may have planted kisses on his neck every now and again or nudged my nose into the back of his hair.

Food had never been so erotic before, and having my dick pressed against his arse didn't help matters any. But I made him do it all; I just helped and instructed, mostly just so I had an excuse to touch him. Or stand with my dick against his arse and my lips at his neck.

By the time we threw it all into a pot, added the minced beef and a jar of sauce, and much to Andrew's dismay, my Aunt Marvie's special ingredient—a few spoonfuls of crushed pineapple—I put the lid on it and set it to simmer.

"Now what?" he asked.

"It needs to cook for a while."

He wiped his hands on a tea towel and set it down on the counter. "For how long? What about the pasta? You know I actually quite enjoyed this. Cooking, that is. It was fun."

I bit my bottom lip and could feel the gravitational pull of every damn centimetre between us. He had no clue how fucking sexy he was or how much he drove me crazy. "Forty-five minutes, maybe an hour, on a real low heat. Plenty of time."

"Plenty of time for what? Pasta doesn't take that long, does it?"

I took two big strides to stand in front of him, so close I spoke against his lips. "Have you forgotten already?"

Recognition sparked in his eyes, and he exhaled in a rush. "Oh. You said after dinner…"

"I did, but for the last half an hour, all I've been doing is imagining how your arse tastes."

He melted against me, like my words made his knees weak. "Oh."

"Do you want me to rim you?" I asked. My lips brushed against his.

He nodded. "I showered," he breathed. "And I cleaned… there."

I smiled and ghosted my lips against his. "I thought you said you'd never done it before."

"I googled," he blurted out.

I chuckled at that. "Did you, now?"

He nodded. "It was very detailed." He cringed. "And kind of gross and explicit. I had to buy some douching bulbs," he said. Then he squinted his eyes closed and made a weird squeaking noise. "Oh my god, I can't believe I just said that."

I put my hands to his face and kissed him. "You are so perfect." I grabbed his hand and led him to my bedroom. When I turned to face him, his expression stopped me. He looked nervous and excited, his cheeks were flushed pink, his lips parted and wet, but his eyes were dark with lust. "Jesus, you're so fucking sexy," I mumbled before I wrapped my hand around his neck and pulled him in for a kiss. He kissed me back, hard and urgent, pawing at my shirt, trying to undress me while never breaking the kiss. He was horny, there was no doubt about it.

"Sit on the bed," I urged him.

His chest was heaving and he looked a little confused, but he did as I told him. I knelt before him and undid his laces, pulled his shoes off, then his socks. I ran my hands up his legs, squeezing his thighs and palming his erection through his trousers. I popped the button on his fly, and he lifted his hips so I could pull his pants down and off him. I tossed them onto the floor and stood up, giving him a close and proper look at the bulge in my pants. I even gave myself a slow palm, more for his benefit than mine. When he looked up at me, he had sex and desire written all over his face.

"Stand up," I whispered. He did, so I pulled his shirt and vest off together and took a long admiring look at his body. "Fuck you're hot."

He undid my jeans roughly. "Maybe we should skip the rimming and move straight to the fucking," he said gruffly.

I grabbed his face and kissed him so hard, ploughing his

mouth with my tongue that he whimpered. He fucking whimpered. "On the bed, face down," I said.

He moved quickly, first kneeling on the bed, then spreading his thighs, he lay down, keeping his arse up. Fuck. He was putting on a show for me. Intentional or not, he was driving me crazy. I wanted so badly to fuck him. I wanted to kneel behind him and bury myself inside him and stay there forever. But I also had to keep true to his wishes of preferring to wait. I was happy to oblige with other acts, but penetrative sex was off-limits for now. Until we discussed it without lust and libido being the driving deciding factor.

I knelt behind him and my rock-hard cock throbbed with need. I think my dick thought it was about to get laid. *Man, I want to...*

Instead, I planted kisses up the backs of his thighs. He writhed, and his splayed his hands out on the bed. "Spencer," he whispered.

His arse was perfect. Pale, toned, rounded, and glorious. He had a blond fuzz lightly dusted over his cheeks, and I licked up one side and gently bit the other. He responded by raising his hips. "Oh God," he mumbled.

I spread his cheeks and softly licked the sensitive skin around his hole, making him bite back a groan. "Can you just..." he started. "Please Spencer, just fuck me."

So I fucked him with my tongue. His reaction was immediate: he squirmed, and half-groaned, half-laughed, and fisted the bedcovers in his hands. "Oh my God."

I pulled my mouth away. "You like it?"

He groaned again. "Yes. Don't stop."

I smiled as I swiped my tongue over his hole. I didn't need him to tell me he liked it; his body's reaction told me all I needed to know. I pushed my tongue into him again, and he moaned as his hips rose to meet me. Fuck, he couldn't get enough. He was so turned on, so damn horny. I couldn't wait until I had my cock in him. He was so responsive, so vocal. I could only imagine the sounds he'd make when he was pounded into the mattress, or better yet, if he did that to me.

He writhed under my hands, under my tongue, and was making the most glorious sounds. He shoved his hand under his hip, no doubt so he could grip his own dick and the thought of him jerking himself off almost did me in. I pulled away and tapped his hip. "Roll over for me," I urged him.

He grumbled about me stopping, but he rolled over and swung his leg up and over so I was again in between his legs. His cock was hard and spilling precum, and he wasted no time in gripping himself.

I slid my briefs down and pulled out my aching cock, humming with relief at the touch. I leaned over him, my thighs between his, and with one hand above his shoulder holding me up, I took both our cocks in my other hand.

Andrew gasped, and his eyes went wide as he fucked my fist. He grabbed my face, but before he kissed me, I pulled my face back and my hand that was rubbing us together slowed. "I've had my mouth on your arse," I said, wanting to remind him that he might not like to kiss that.

His nostrils flared, and he pulled my face to his, kissing me deeply. So fucking deeply. I almost forgot to keep pumping our dicks until he bucked his hips up, and he groaned into my mouth as he came.

Feeling him surge and swell in my hand, against my own cock, sent me over the edge, and my orgasm uncurled through me. When the room had stopped spinning and I finally opened my eyes, Andrew was staring at me. "God, Spencer..."

I collapsed on top of him and laughed into his neck. "You're welcome."

His chest vibrated under me as he chuckled. "Why are you still completely dressed and I'm very naked?"

"I meant to get undressed," I said, pulling back so I could see his face. I rested my head on my hand and sighed. "But you were too fucking gorgeous."

He burst out laughing and blushed right down his neck. "That was intense, that's for sure."

"Not that I really need to ask because I know the answer already, but how was your first rimming experience?"

He laughed some more and put his hand over his eyes, embarrassed. I peeled his hand away so he'd look at me. "Don't be embarrassed, Andrew. You have no idea how much you turned me on."

His lip pulled down. "Oh."

He seriously had no clue how fucking sexy he was. "I mean it. I could literally eat you with a spoon."

"Well, that would probably hurt."

I snorted out a laugh. "We better get cleaned up."

"How about you go check on dinner and I just lay here," he said. "I'm pretty blissed out right now, and I don't even know if my legs'll work."

I laughed, then thought about what he said. "Shit. Dinner." I scampered off him, then the bed, and tripped over myself into the living room as I fixed my trousers. I stirred the bolognaise sauce and filled the largest pot with water and put it on the stove to boil. Next, I went to the bathroom, cleaned myself up, wet a washer with warm water, and walked back to my room. Andrew was still laying there, arms and legs spread wide with the sheet pulled to his waist. Despite how incredible he looked still naked in my bed, the smirk on his face was my favourite thing. "Do you have any intention of getting out of that bed?"

His smile widened. "No."

I tossed the washer at him, and it landed on his stomach. "Ah!" he cried, flailing. Then he stopped. "Oh, it's warm."

I laughed and ran and jumped on him, kneeling over him with my hands on either side of his head. I leaned down and kissed him.

"Mm, minty," he said.

"Mouthwash. You know, considering what I ate last."

It took him a second. "Oh my God."

"It really embarrasses you, doesn't it?"

"Of course it does! You're talking about eating my…"

"Arse?" I sat back, effectively straddling his hips. "And it was delicious."

He threw the washer at my face, then covered his own with his hands. "Jesus, Spencer."

I laughed and wiped the washer over his stomach and chest. "Don't be embarrassed. It's just us."

His hands fell away, and he looked at me. It was as though my words flipped a switch in his head. He looked at me for a long moment. "Just us, huh?"

"Yep." I shuffled down a bit and pulled the sheet away so I could clean him up properly. He was half hard again, his cock lay thick and snug across his hip. "You have the most gorgeous cock I think I've ever seen."

He laughed again and shook his head. He didn't cover his eyes so I considered it a win. "Seen many?" he asked.

"A few. I told you when we first met, I love arse, and I love dick."

"True. You did say that."

"I've always had safe sex though, and I've been tested regularly."

"Oh." He blinked, my change in conversational direction clearly shocked him. "Um, me too."

I wiped him over thoroughly, relishing in the weight of

his dick in my hand, and tossed the washer onto the floor. He cleared his throat. "Can I ask you something?"

"Of course." I couldn't resist, so I edged back up to straddle his hips. I was fully dressed, but he was still stark naked. "Ask me anything."

"If I told you your clothes were offending me right now, would you take them off?"

I leaned down and kissed him softly. "I thought you were about to ask a serious question."

He put his hands on my thighs and lifted his hips a little. "It was serious," he said. His eyes were alight with mischief. "I have to admit, the view from here is pretty damn amazing."

I wiggled my arse on his lengthening dick. "View ain't bad from here either."

He bit his lip. "How long are we gonna wait?" he asked.

Jesus. He was so eager for it. "I'm taking my cues from you," I said. "I don't want you to regret it."

He laughed. "Regret it? God, Spencer, it's all I can think about."

I rubbed my arse on his cock. "I can feel that."

He put his head back and groaned. "I'm trying to be good. I just wanted us to talk more and not end up in bed all the time, but"—he waved his hand at the bed—"that hasn't really worked out."

I laughed. "How about we make it till the weekend at least."

"But that's so far away." He pouted. "Next time I have these great ideas about abstinence, please tell me to wake up to myself."

I kissed him with smiling lips. "We're hardly abstaining, considering what we just did. We're just treading cautiously."

He made a thoughtful face, then cocked his head. "What's that sound?"

I listened. It sounded like it was coming from the kitchen. "Shit. Dinner." I jumped off him and ran out to find the pot of water boiling furiously.

Apparently all Andrew could do was laugh. He called out, "See? This is why I order in!"

"Have you had a guy in your bed distracting you every night of the week for most of your adult life?" I called back to him.

He replied, "Only the most memorable ones."

"Well, for your information, I'm putting the spaghetti in the boiling water. You know, so when you cook this for me next time, you'll know what to do."

It took a moment, but he walked out of my room with his pants on and pulled his shirt over his head. "Me? Cook for you?"

"Yep."

He went to the bathroom, and a minute or two later when he came back out, he walked over to where I was at the stove and looked at the pasta sticking out of the pot. "I've told you before, I don't cook. But shouldn't that be *in* the water?"

God, he made me laugh. "Have you seriously never cooked spaghetti? It needs to soften."

He shrugged at the pot before pulling me in and kissing my cheek, smelling all minty too. He must have used my mouthwash. "I have never cooked spaghetti."

"Jesus. How did you survive college?"

"I lived at home."

"Did your parents never teach you?"

"They tried. When I burned some expensive pot, my mom made me promise I wouldn't try again."

"You weren't allowed to cook after you burned a pot?"

"Well, that and some of the kitchen."

I think my mouth fell open. I was speechless.

He shrugged. "It wasn't a big deal. Mom wanted to remodel anyway."

I couldn't help but laugh. "Well, in that case, when you cook for me, it might be best if you wait for me to get there."

He rolled his eyes. "Want me to set the table? I think I can manage that."

I kissed him. "Thank you."

While we ate dinner, he asked about my new client, and I told him everything. I didn't want him to think I was doing anything behind his back, and if this whole actual-boyfriend-thing was going to work when my job was to have fake-boyfriends, I needed Andrew to know every detail.

"But you couldn't find this guy?"

I shook my head. "Not really. He's moved address and changed jobs. He has no Facebook, not that I could find. Even Lance the Tosser said his profile is gone. Sounds like his parents made him cut all ties."

Andrew frowned, probably knowing this case sounded a little too close to home for me. "Do you think he's okay?"

"I have no clue. Lola has a job in town tomorrow so she's going to drop me off at the college. I'll look around, see what I can find out. If it comes up empty, I'll contact Lance and tell him it's a no-deal."

"Then what will you do?"

"Move onto the next job."

"Just like that?"

"Sure. I had a message on my phone today from a prospective client. I'm never out of work for long. I called him back and got his voice mail."

He made a face that was hard to read. "I had lunch with my mother today."

Oh. *Random subject change, but okay.* "How'd that go?"

"Oh good," he said, a fond look upon his face. "She

wanted to know all about you. She'd seen the photos of course, and Sarah told her I had a new boyfriend."

Well, this could go any direction. "And what did you tell her?"

"That you're Australian, and that you're incredibly good-looking," he said. "That if there was a magazine called *Aussies Living Sexy in LA*, you'd be on the cover."

I snorted. "Really?"

"Yep. She argued that Hugh Jackman or Chris Hemsworth would be on the cover, and I just laughed at her. I said, 'Wait till you see him,' and then of course she asked when she would... see you, that is."

"Oh."

He chuckled quietly. "Don't worry. I told her 'When we're ready for that.' No pressure."

I was relieved, I couldn't deny it. Meeting parents—meeting anyone's parents—and hoping for their approval was not something I did well. I wiped my hands on my thighs and swallowed hard. "I just struggle with parents and acceptance, that's all. It's nothing against your folks, and it's not indicative of what I think of *us* in any way."

Andrew reached over and put his hand on my arm. "I know that. It's fine. She was completely understanding. I told her I was trying to take things slower with you and that meeting the parents wasn't conducive to taking things slow."

"And was she okay with that?"

"Yes, more than okay. She said it was a good thing I was trying to put the brakes on a little."

"Oh."

Andrew laughed. "It wasn't about you," he said. "It was more about me not diving in head first like I normally do." He collected our empty plates and took them into the kitchen. He put them in the sink and turned to face me. "She asked what you did for a living."

Oh.

"I told her exactly what you do. I said you're like a relationship fixer," he said. "I told her exactly how we met, that it was originally a ploy to get Eli back."

I swallowed down the lump in my throat. "And what did she say to that?"

Andrew shrugged. "Not much. She never really liked Eli."

I snorted. "Did anyone?"

He pulled a face at me. "Anyway," he continued, "my point about telling my mother what it is you do, is that I don't have a problem with what you do for a job. I'm not hiding any part of you to anyone. I told Michelle, my friend at work, what you did for a job, and she thought it was cute. But I've always been a firm believer that what we do for work doesn't define us. I draw cartoons for a living, but it's not who I am. You're no different."

I swallowed thickly. He understood me so damn well, and my honesty was the least I could offer him. "Can I tell you something?"

"Of course."

"I don't *need* to be a relationship-fixer."

He tilted his head, his brows knitted together. "I don't want you to be something you're not. I just said that."

I almost smiled. "No, what I mean is, I don't actually need to do anything for a job. I have—" I swallowed hard, not overly comfortable telling anyone this. "—money."

He blinked.

"When I said my Aunt Marvie left me a chunk of money, I wasn't kidding. I just don't tell many people. It's invested and in term deposits so I don't have a huge cash flow, but I live off the interest, basically. And I live here because I love it. Sure it's small and whatever, but it's close to Emilio and Lola, and I don't need material things to make me happy. But I don't do what I do for the money. I do it because I like helping people."

Andrew stared at me, then he laughed. "You are an interesting man, Spencer."

"You don't care?"

"Why would I care? I said it doesn't bother me what you do for a job."

I was talking about the money, but he didn't even seem to care about that either. I stood up from the table and walked over to him. I put my hand to his face and kissed him softly. "You're kind of great, you know that?"

He smiled all shyly. "Did you say you got gelato?"

I let out a laugh and put my hand on his flat stomach. "Where do you put it all?"

"Yeah, don't worry. At this rate I'll be at the gym at 4:00 a.m."

So, with the tub of gelato and two spoons, we planted our arses in front of the TV and watched re-runs of *Family Feud* until almost midnight, laughing and arguing about who was winning and taking the piss out of each other's answers.

He texted me when he got home.

> Had the best night, thank you.

Me too.

> My place, Thursday night?

Will you cook?

> If I have to. Oh, sorry, damn autocorrect.
> That was supposed to be If you help me.

LOL. Deal.

Talk tomorrow?

Of course.

Night, Spencer. Sweet dreams.

I was still smiling when Lola picked me up the next morning.

SEVEN

I climbed into Cindy Crawford, Lola's 80s model car, and Lola swerved back into traffic before I could even put our drinks into the cup-holder and put my seat belt on. We'd gone a block when I handed her her coffee. She eyed me instead of the road. "Look at you all smug smiles. I take it things with Andrew are going great?"

"Can you watch the traffic? I don't feel like dying today."

She smiled, sipped her coffee, changed gears, and changed lanes one handed, and all while looking at me. I didn't really need the green tea when I had a morning heart-starter like a trip in the car with Lola at the wheel.

"So?" she pressed. "I take it you and Andrew...?"

"We still haven't had sex," I told her.

She swerved, a car honked its horn, and she straightened up. "What do you mean? You're definitely getting something. I can tell."

I laughed. "Well, true. We're... fooling around, doing some stuff, but no penetrative sex. Yet."

"Can I ask why? I mean, statistically gay men have the most sex out of everyone, so you're singlehandedly ruining the bell curve, honey. It's going to look more like a Smurf hat than a bell, Spence. Do you want that on your conscience?"

I almost spat my tea. "Just because it's not actual fucking, doesn't mean it's not sex. We're doing our part to prop up the bell curve, believe me. We're taking things slower so we don't fizzle and burn out, that's all." Then I noticed the cars in front of us were stopped, but Lola was still looking at me. I put my free hand on the dash. "Ah, Lola?"

She hit the brakes, and without missing a beat, she said, "Aww, that's so sweet."

I took a calming breath. "Remind me next time to have my tea with a Xanax to go."

"I thought you were going to tell me he was saving himself."

"Ah, no. He's finding it harder to abstain than me, I think."

"I ain't surprised. Look at you. Looking all dapper today."

I was wearing my navy blue three-quarter pants, a white T-shirt, and Andrew's Argyle vest that he left at my place. "Andrew told his mother I would be on the cover of *Aussies Living Sexy in LA.*"

She grinned, her eyes wide. "He does the fake magazine cover thing too?"

"Yep."

"Awww, see? You're a match made in heaven!"

I laughed. "You like his vest on me? He left it at my place last night."

"It suits you," she said, again looking at me and not the road.

"Um, car. Car!"

Lola slowed down so we didn't rear end the car in front of us, thankfully. "So, you're going to an acting school in search of a guy you can't find?"

"Yeah. I have no clue what this one's about. If I can't find a trace of him after today, I'll just tell Lance it was a no-go."

"Oh, did a Peter Hannikov call you?"

"Yes, he left a message. You know him?"

"He's a friend of a lady Gabe works with. He split with his boyfriend. It's all rather sad apparently, but Mindy, who works with Gabe, suggested calling you. Could be worth a shot."

I smiled. "Thanks. I called him back and left a message. I'll try again today."

We came up to the acting school and Lola pulled Cindy Crawford up to the kerb. "I'll bus it home; thank you for the lift."

"No worries," she replied.

"Oh, and it's still my shout for dinner. Does Friday night sound good? I'll order something in for everyone at the shop, say around nine? Emilio should be shut by then."

"Sounds great!"

I jumped out of the car and barely had the door shut before Lola took off into traffic. I watched until she'd disappeared, amazed at how she even got a licence, then turned to face the college.

The school of visual and performing arts was huge. It was a grey building on a campus, of sorts, with trees and wide welcoming steps at the front. There were people milling about. Students, obviously. Young, wearing jeans and backpacks, most of who were laughing and talking animatedly with their hands, clearly happy to be at a school they wanted to be in. I somehow couldn't imagine students who studied maths or law being so vivacious.

Not that I knew for certain, because I'd never gone to college—I'd never wanted to. But I was unremarkable here. I walked into the school grounds like I belonged. No one would look at me twice and wonder what I was lurking around for. Not that I had any intention of lurking at the school; I knew I wouldn't get far with random questions to strangers about a fellow student. There was a group of five, three guys, two girls, standing near the steps, all smiling as they talked, and I approached them.

"I was wondering if you could help me?" I interrupted. "I was told the best coffee shop was Grand something?" Given my Australian accent and my request for directions, I let them assume I was a new student here.

One of the guys pointed left. "Grand Café. About half a block that way."

"Cheers," I said, giving them all a smile as I went in the direction he offered.

I couldn't stand at the steps with a photo of Yanni asking if anyone had seen him without raising suspicions and possibly scoring myself a meeting with campus security, so I figured the coffee shop he worked at would be the best place to start. My phone call to the café hadn't gotten me anywhere, but maybe a meeting face to face would.

The café was busy, students grabbing a last minute caffeine hit before class mostly but a few suits as well. I hung back and waited until the line died down a bit, to give myself more time to speak to the girl behind the counter. I had no idea if it was the same girl I spoke to on the phone, and in all honesty, I wasn't expecting to get any information.

I ordered my green tea, and seeing they had boxes of some varieties for sale, I used that as my conversation opener. "What are the different ones you have there?" I asked.

"Green tea with honey, green tea with lemon, green tea with orange," she said, bringing a box of each over. "They're new."

I smelled each box, just to see if I could get a hint of any scent. I put the orange one aside. "I'll take this one, thanks."

"No worries," she replied.

Her name tag declared her to be Jing. A small Asian girl who seemed cheerful and pleasant enough, and seeing she was alone behind the counter for a moment, I handed her some cash and said, "I phoned yesterday, I'm not sure if it was you I spoke to. I'm looking for Yanni. He's a friend of mine, and I'm worried about him."

She looked at me before she scanned the room for her co-workers, somewhat nervously. She handed me my change, and said, "If you take a seat, I'll bring your tea over."

"Great, thanks." I found a seat toward the back and waited. Only by the time my tea was ready, her two colleagues were close by. Not intentionally, just cleaning tables and chatting with nearby customers. But when Jing delivered my tea, I knew it wasn't the right time.

"Thank you," I said with a smile. She looked around nervously again, so before she could clam up, I told her, "I'll hang around the campus for about an hour. Out the front, under the trees. If you have something you can share."

She blinked a few times, wiping the table down before nodding, ever so slightly, and going back to the counter.

I finished my tea, collected my box of tealeaves, and went back to the college to wait.

And wait. And wait.

I gave her an hour, then I gave her another. I liked to people-watch so I didn't mind. It was pleasant enough in the shade, and most people gave me a smile as they walked past. I was just about to give up when Jing came scurrying around the corner. She saw me and slowed to a walk, nervously sitting on the same seat. "I had to stay late, sorry. I thought you might be gone."

"Thanks for coming," I said.

"Yanni was my friend," she said. "We weren't close, but he was nice to me. I worry about him too."

"Have you seen him lately?"

She shook her head. "Last time I saw him was two weeks ago. He came into work to tell Sasha—he's our boss—that he couldn't work anymore."

"Did he say why?"

She looked at me then. "No, but he was all banged up. He had a black eye and a cut on his cheek."

Oh, Jesus. I literally sagged. "Oh, no."

"He wouldn't say who did it," Jing said quietly. "Just that he had moved and changed schools also."

"Had he ever mentioned his family to you?" I asked. "If his parents were strict or religious or anything like that?"

She shook her head. "No. He never spoke of them."

I'd already sounded too much like an interviewer and not like a concerned friend. "He just told me once they weren't cool with a lot of things. They were pretty hard on him."

"Because he's gay?" she asked.

I nodded. "Mostly. Did he tell you about Lance? They'd been dating each other for a while."

Jing shook her head. "No. I gathered he was seeing someone, but we didn't talk about that stuff. Have you spoken to him, the boyfriend?"

"Yeah. He hasn't heard from him either."

She frowned. "Oh. Well, that's not good."

I leaned back and sighed, certain this was another dead end. "Thank you for talking to me, Jing. I appreciate your help."

"Do you think you'll find him?"

I looked at her and answered honestly. "I don't think he

wants to be found right now. He's changed his phone, jobs, schools, and didn't tell anyone where he was going."

"Do you think he's okay?"

I looked her right in the eye. "I hope so."

Jing stood up. She looked as though she was warring with a decision in her head. "I um, I don't know if I should tell you this... but I can see in your eyes you are concerned."

That wasn't pretend. The more I heard about Yanni, the more I was concerned. "Tell me what?"

"I heard he went to Pol's, but I don't know if that's true."

"Pol's?"

Her eyes narrowed a little. "You know, Pol's Academy."

"Oh, of course. Sorry, of course." I had no clue what she was talking about, but under my pretence of being a friend who had classes with Yanni, I realised a little too late that I should have known such things. I scrubbed my hand over my face. "I'll try there. Thank you so much."

She walked a few steps from me, then stopped. "If you find him. Tell him I said hi."

I smiled at her. "I will. Thank you." I sat there for a little while longer, turning my phone over in my hands, wondering what on earth I was going to tell Lance. He was strictly my boss for this job, and I owed it to him to tell him what I'd found. I never promised him good news.

I went through my contacts, found his number and dialled. I wasn't surprised it went through to voicemail but didn't want to leave news of Yanni having a black eye over the phone. "Lance, It's Spencer Cohen. I might have found something on Yanni, though it could be another dead end. I'll need to follow it up. It's the last hope I've got. I'll be in touch as soon as I know."

I took the next bus home and spent the afternoon helping Emilio in the shop, grateful for the distraction.

EIGHT

I SPENT THE NEXT MORNING DOING SOME RESEARCH on Pol's. Which, as it turned out to be was a smaller acting school. From what Google street view showed me, it looked like an ordinary storefront on some backstreet and not like a school or college at all. It was the polar opposite of the college Yanni used to go to.

Was this his parents' compromise? Was this his punishment?

It was hard to put any pieces of the puzzle together for a guy I'd never met or even laid eyes on for that matter. I called Lance again, and this time he answered.

"Spencer," he answered.

"Yeah. I left a message yesterday."

"Yes, I worked late," he explained. "Sorry I missed you. You found something?"

"I'm not sure, to be honest. Can we meet?" I asked. I didn't want to have this conversation over the phone.

"I've got appointments all day—" I heard voices in the background. Lance said something to them that sounded like "Be there in five minutes" and then he spoke back into the phone. "—which are about to start actually. I won't be done until after dinnertime. Can we talk now?"

"Sure. I went to his old school and spoke to someone he used to work with."

He paused a moment. "And?"

"No one has seen him."

He sighed into the phone. "Oh."

"I know. It's like he's disappeared."

"You have a lead though?"

"I do. It could turn out to be nothing. I just wanted you to know that I'm still trying, but this is it. If I turn up nothing in the next day or so, I'll call us done."

He cleared his throat. "That's a shame."

"Well, it's not exactly a typical case I'm used to. I haven't even seen this guy."

"I just want to know what happened to him."

"Yeah, I get that. And I'm sorry to have to tell you this, but the co-worker I spoke to said the last time they saw him, he'd been touched up. He had a black eye. That was the day he quit his job."

I heard a faint gasp, then silence.

"Lance?"

There was a ruffling sound, like he'd changed which ear he was listening with and then, "Did he tell them who did it?"

"No."

"What's your lead?" he asked. "What are you looking into?"

I don't know why I hesitated, and I don't know why I lied, but the words were out before I could stop them. "Someone thought they saw him working in a bookstore in town. I'll go in, see if I can find him or ask some other staff if they know him. It's a long shot, but it's all I've got."

"Which bookstore?"

"Barnes & Noble at The Grove," I lied smoothly. I chose it because it was huge and non-descript, so it wouldn't be too easy to call my bullshit if he decided to go check it out himself. "That's all I know."

"Okay, I have to go."

"I'll call you tomorrow."

"Do that."

He disconnected the call. I clicked off my phone and slid it across the table. "Arsehole," I muttered to myself before going downstairs to see if Emilio or Daniela needed me to do anything and was still grumbling about him half an hour later. "The guy's a jerk. I'm in half a mind to find this Yanni guy and congratulate him on dumping his arse."

Emilio didn't even look up from where he was inking some guy. He just snorted out a laugh. "Tell us what you really think, man."

Daniela was more concerned. "But you think he is in danger?"

I shrugged. "I don't know. He was last seen with a black eye before he quit work and school. Lance said its Yanni's father."

"But?"

"But I don't know. There was something about Lance I didn't like from the second I saw him. You know that voice in your head that tells you something's not right?" I asked.

Daniela nodded furiously. "Yes. Your sixth sense."

I continued, "Well, at first I put it down to this guy being too rich for his own good, arrogant and self-serving, thinking he could buy people, which I hate even on a good day. But what if it's more than that? What if *he* gave Yanni the black eye? What if Yanni left him for good reason?"

Now Emilio sat up and stopped tattooing. "You think so?"

"I don't know." I sighed. "I don't know what to make of it. When I told him Yanni had a black eye, the first thing he asked was if Yanni had said who did it. Not if he was okay, or *oh my God*, or anything."

Daniela frowned. "What will you do?"

"I told Lance Yanni was seen working in town."

Emilio's eyes narrowed. "You told him where he works?"

"No. I have no clue where Yanni works. I had to tell him something. And I'm going to head in town tonight to stake out the bookstore I said Yanni worked at and see if Lance turns up. You know, to see if he's a psycho stalker or not."

Emilio's smile was slow and wide. "Good thinking."

"You be careful," Daniela said.

"I will. I was thinking I could take Andrew and make a bit of a date out of it." Truthfully, I only just thought of it, but the more I considered it, the more it seemed like a great idea.

Daniela stared at me like I'd lost my mind. "You want to take Andrew on a date to check out a real-life, psycho stalker?"

"Yes, but I'll buy him a book, and ooh!" I said, flipping through the local gig guide as a new idea struck, "I should see if there's a jazz bar in town. I promised him I'd take him, and I haven't yet."

Emilio, who had gone back to inking his client, said, "You're buying him books and taking him to jazz bars?"

"Yeah. So?"

He didn't look up, but I could tell he was smiling. "You wanna be careful, Spencer. That boy might wanna marry you."

ALL JOKES ASIDE, I TEXTED ANDREW.

> You busy tonight?

He replied about an hour later, in what I assumed was his lunch break. By that time I had cleaned floors, tidied the waiting area, and checked my phone only about two hundred times.

> Depends. I was going to order salad for dinner, play some vinyl records my sexy boyfriend gave me, and settle in for some single-handed loving. Does that count as busy?

I chuckled as I replied.

> No, it counts as hot, but not busy. And I'm pretty sure you'd need both hands. Your dick's pretty big.

> LOL Did you want to do something?

> I want to take you on a date. To a bookstore and a jazz bar. Is that okay?

> Michelle wants to know why I just laughed and hugged my phone. JSYK, I didn't hug it. She tells lies.

Michelle was a girl he worked with, and over the last few years, they'd become the best of friends. I'd heard him talk of her in passing, but I'd never met her. Actually, I'd never met any of his friends.

> Tell her I said hi.

She says hi back. She wants to know if you have any old tattoo magazines she could borrow. She wants to get her first tattoo.

For sure! I'll bring some tonight. She should come see Emilio.

That's what I told her.

I'll see you at six?

Can't wait.

I sighed happily and pocketed my phone, then I noticed that Emilio and even his client were now watching me. "What?"

Emilio nodded slowly. "Oh yeah, you have it bad, my friend."

Just then, Lola pushed her way backwards through the front door, her arms full of boxes. I was quick to grab some before she dropped them. "They're picking on me," I told her.

She straightened up and composed herself to her usual glamorous self. "How so?"

Emilio laughed, still inking the guy in the chair. "He's got it bad for Andrew. He was just smiling at his phone like he'd just found out his favourite porn site had waived his subscription fees."

"See?" I told Lola. "They're taking the piss."

"But honey, it's not taking the piss if it's true."

They all laughed, and I sighed in defeat. "And I suppose you want me to help you with all these?" I held up the boxes I'd taken from her.

"Of course." She smiled beautifully. Her soft lipstick

matched the colour of her hair. "So tell me, what's the latest with Andrew?"

"He's got a hot date tonight," Daniela called out from the back cubicle. "He's taking him to stalk a psycho in a bookstore, then to a jazz club."

Lola looked at me with one perfectly shaped eyebrow raised. "Stalking psychos? I haven't seen you for one morning, Spence. One morning. What the hell did I miss?"

After I'd explained everything and helped her sort colour palettes of eyeshadows, blushes, and lipsticks, I explained how I had hoped to find Yanni at Pol's acting studio as a last ditch effort.

"I can drive you tomorrow," she said.

"It's in the afternoon. I checked the website and classes on Thursdays are later than other days."

"Perfect. Suits me better, actually. And then you can help me on Friday. I've got a job in Pasadena. Should only be a few hours. That okay?"

"Perfect."

IT WAS RIDICULOUS HOW EXCITED I WAS ABOUT tonight. It was just a trip to a bookstore and then to a jazz bar, but it was our first official date out together. It was going to be a perfect night. Apart from stalking the psycho, that I didn't know whether he was an actual psycho, and I didn't know if he was even going to show up. I hoped all kinds of hope that he wouldn't show, because that would mean he wasn't the psycho I got the feeling he was, and because then I could make the whole night about Andrew.

I was dressed and ready to go, looking as good as I got, just after five. "Looking at your watch every thirty seconds won't make the time pass any quicker," Lola said. She was almost done for the day, and I was getting antsy, apparently.

"It's ridiculous, isn't it?" I asked. "I'm being ridiculous, aren't I?

She grinned at me and grabbed her handbag. "Not at all. Come on, I'll drive you."

"He probably won't be home yet anyway, and his neighbour already thinks I'm some wacko. I'm pretty sure she was gonna mace me."

"Well, good for her. If you were some wacko, she should mace you."

"That's what I told Andrew."

Lola laughed at that. "You're adorable."

We got into Cindy Crawford, and this time when I buckled my seatbelt, I tried to be inconspicuous when I did a small sign of the cross on my forehead, but Lola saw me do it. "Did you just say a prayer?"

"Maybe."

She gasped. "Because of my driving?"

"Possibly."

"Do you do that every time you get in my car?"

"Um..."

She put Cindy in reverse and grinded the gears before pulling out of her parking spot. "Spencer Cohen, I'm deeply offended."

"I think of it more as a sign of faith," I explained as she turned out of the lot into traffic at warp speed. "That you scare the shit out of me, yet I still willingly get in this car."

"I'm not a bad driver," she declared.

"No, you're a very good driver," I agreed. "Considering the speed you drive and the total lack of consideration for other drivers or physics in general."

She glared at me.

"Please look at the road," I told her. "I don't feel like dying today. Or being seriously injured."

"Oh," she sang sarcastically. "It's all about personal safety now that you've got a boyfriend."

I laughed at her. "Yes, that's totally the reason I don't want to die today."

She sighed dramatically. "I see how it is."

"You know I love you."

She swerved lanes like a race car driver and stopped at a red light. "Well, I just don't know..." She sniffed.

"Did I tell you you look particularly gorgeous today?"

She couldn't hold it in any longer. She laughed. "You're a shit."

"I know."

We pulled into Andrew's street and his car was out front of his house. "Oh, he's home already."

"Did you text him to let him know you were coming early?"

"Nope. I was going for spontaneous."

"You were going for 'Shit, I forgot.'"

"That too." Smiling, I took her hand off the wheel, kissed her knuckles like the gentleman I was. "Thank you for the lift."

She rolled her eyes. "Sorry you thought you were going to die."

"See you tomorrow?"

"Yes. And I want all the details. All of them."

I climbed out, tattoo magazines in hand, and waited for her to drive off. I crossed the street, happily humming to myself, and pressed Andrew's doorbell. My ridiculous smile died when it wasn't Andrew who opened the door. I'd never met this person before in my life. Hell, I'd never even seen photos, but I knew exactly who it was because they looked so damned alike.

Andrew's mother smiled at me. "You must be Spencer."

NINE

Stuck for the right thing to say, wanting to run but knowing I shouldn't, my useless brain spoke without me. "You're really pretty."

She threw her head back and laughed, and I wanted to die. Literally die. In that split second, I wished I was still in the car with Lola, careening through traffic at sixty miles per hour, waving merrily at death every other block.

Instead my stupid feet stayed stuck to the floor, and my stupid mouth just kept on going. Because seriously, why stop at embarrassed when mortified was so much more fun. "For a woman, I mean."

"Spencer?" Andrew came out from the hall. "You're early."

Oh, thank God. "Help me because I have a stupid brain."

Now he laughed, and his mother, I was absolutely certain, thought I was an idiot. She was clearly amused, delighted even, and I was still standing at the door. Andrew, biting his lip to stop the grin on his face from getting any bigger, dragged me inside. His mother was just like him: tall, lean, graceful, and she held herself with poise. She was impeccably dressed in a flowy green top and crisp white pants with enough gold jewellery to be elegant without being pretentious. She didn't need to remind people she was classy; it was in the air around her. "Spencer, this is my mom, Helen. Mom, this is Spencer."

"Nice to meet you," Helen said gracefully. "Andrew warned me to leave before you got here, but you're early."

"I am, sorry. Lola offered me a lift, and taking Cindy Crawford is better than a bus, even if it means almost dying."

They both stared at me. Andrew put his arm around me and chuckled. "Mom, Cindy Crawford is Lola's car."

She put her hand to her heart. "Oh."

Dear God, this couldn't get any worse. "I'm really sorry. Can we start over?" I held out my hand. "I'm Spencer Cohen. It's lovely to meet you. I'm not usually such an idiot. Just nervous."

Helen shook my hand with a fond smile. "It's very nice to meet you. Please don't be nervous. Andrew explained you would be, hence my being cautioned to not be here. He tells me you're taking him to a bookstore and jazz bar?"

"Yes, ma'am."

She sighed dramatically. "A man after my own heart."

"Okay, Mom," Andrew urged.

"Yes, yes," she said, collecting her designer label handbag from the sofa. She kissed Andrew's cheek, he promised to call her, and she looked at me once more. "It's very nice to meet you, Spencer. You're as handsome and charming as Andrew said you were."

I could feel my face heat with embarrassment, and Andrew ushered his mother to the door. When she was gone, he leaned against the door and exhaled. "I'm really sorry."

"Don't you apologise," I said. "I'm the one who turned up unannounced!"

Andrew made a frowny, uncertain face. "It wasn't too bad, was it?"

"I told her she was really pretty," I explained, still horrified. "For a woman."

Andrew laughed and walked over to me. He put his hand on my waist. "For what it's worth, I think she likes you."

"I have a stupid brain that says ridiculous things."

He leaned up and kissed my forehead. "You keep saying you have a stupid brain, but I must disagree."

I sighed. "Did you really tell her I was handsome and charming?"

He kissed me softly. "Yep. I can't lie to my mother."

I took a deep breath and tried to look at the bright side. "Well, at least it's done now, I guess."

He snorted. "You make it sound like a vaccination or a rectal exam."

I laughed at that. "I'm not opposed to needles," I said, pulling my sleeve up to show him my tattoos. "And I happen to love rectal exams."

"I knew as soon as I said that where your mind would go."

Still smiling, I handed him the folded magazines. "For Michelle."

"Oh, thanks. She'll love them." He took them and slid them onto the dining table. "So, why the long sleeves?"

"I don't always show off my tatts," I said.

"I've only ever seen you wear your sleeves rolled or a T-shirt," he went on to say.

"Don't you like what I'm wearing?" I looked down at my light blue button down shirt, dark jeans, and my favourite blue loafers. "I thought I did pretty good today."

He hummed, and walking back over to me, he slid his hand around my neck and kissed me. "You look hot. You always look hot."

I licked my lips at the lingering taste of him. "Mmm. And you taste good."

He slid his hand down over his crotch and readjusted himself. "Goddammit. I seem to have this reoccurring problem when you're around."

I waggled my eyebrows at him. "I'm more than happy to help you out with that." I pushed him over to the piano so his back was pressed against it, and I licked my lips. "Before I do this, you should know something." This could be a mood killer, but I didn't want to get side-tracked. "There's another reason I'm wearing my sleeves rolled down."

"What's that?"

"Tattoos are distinguishable. People remember seeing them. I want to go to the bookstore in town tonight because I told Lance the Tosser that's where Yanni worked, and I want to see if he turns up."

Andrew tilted his head, his brows furrowed. "So, it's not really a date for me?"

"Yes it is. It's just an added bonus that I get to take you, and then the jazz bar is all for you."

"Why don't you want Lance the Tosser to turn up at the bookstore?"

"I think he's the reason Yanni disappeared."

Andrew blinked. "Really?"

"I can't be sure." I then explained my trip to the college in town and how Yanni was seen with a black eye, my resulting phone call to Lance, and just the skin-crawling feeling I got from him.

Andrew was thoughtful for moment. "So you're taking me on a covert operation to see if your client is really an asshole."

"Yes."

"And if he is?"

"Then we cross that bridge when we get to it."

He nodded slowly. "Right."

I took a step back. "Am I forgiven?"

"Nope," he said, then he palmed his dick again. "I believe you were about to help me with this."

"I won't be forgiven unless I suck your dick?"

He blushed or was turned on. It was hard to tell the difference. "It's a start."

Smiling, I dropped to my knees, undid his fly, and pulled out his hardening dick. I looked up at him to find him leaning back with his elbows on the piano, looking back down at me. His eyes were fixed on mine, his mouth hanging open, waiting, anticipating... It was fucking hot.

Without breaking eye contact, I opened my mouth, flattened my tongue, and took him in. His whole body reacted, flinched and writhed, and his eyes fluttered closed. It might have been a start, but I finished him in no time.

WE CABBED IT INTO THE CITY, WHICH WAS RATHER uneventful. Andrew told me about his day, I told him about mine, and before long, we were downtown. We got out of the cab and started walking up toward the bookstore, when Andrew stopped.

"What's up?" I asked.

"Can I hold your hand?"

It was funny how simple words could make your heart trip over itself. "Um, yes?" I said. I was pretty sure I was wearing that ridiculous smile again.

Andrew exhaled deeply. "I just wanted to ask. Some people don't like it; some people are too afraid that some random stranger will make a big deal of seeing two guys holding hands. Some people are just not hand-holders, and that's okay. I never asked you before if you liked to hold—"

"Andrew?"

"Yes?"

I put mine out, palm up, between us. "Shut up and hold my hand."

He smiled but kind of growled as he entwined our fingers. "I still haven't forgiven you for the ruse to take me to a bookstore. It's like a fake-date."

"It's not a fake-date," I protested. I leaned in and whispered as we walked, "But I could blow you in the bathrooms at the bookstore if you want. You know, to be forgiven."

He went red from his forehead down under his collar. He looked around as if someone walking near us might have heard. "Spencer!"

I pretended like it was no big deal, because it wasn't, and squeezed his fingers. "This is nice. I think I like going on dates and holding hands."

He stopped walking and stared at me, causing the people behind us to balk and have to sidestep us. "Sorry," he said to them and pulled me to the wall out of the flow of traffic. He looked concerned, or confused, possibly both. "Have you ever walked down the street holding a guy's hand? I mean, for real?"

I shook my head. "Nope."

He sighed and his shoulders fell. "I'm sorry, I should have realised. I shouldn't have been so blasé about it."

"You weren't blasé. In fact, you asked me if it was okay, and that was kinda nice."

"Are you comfortable in doing it?"

I wanted to tell him it was no big deal, but in all honesty, it was. It shouldn't be. But it was. Some gay guys would never do it, for fear of retribution, unwanted attention, and other general arseholeness from the world. The fact Andrew was confident in himself to do it, and the fact he wanted to hold *my* hand, was a big deal.

"Yes, I am. And thank you for asking. It's another first for me, that I can cross off my 'Because of Andrew' list."

"You have a 'Because of what' list?"

"Because of you list. Like if I can finish any sentence with 'because of Andrew,' it goes on the list."

He chuckled. "Do I want to know?"

"Sure. Like now. I have my first real boyfriend because of Andrew," I explained. "Or, I now smile like an idiot all the time because of Andrew."

He laughed. "Do I want to know what's number one on this list?"

"I jerk off five times a day because of Andrew," I said. He cracked up laughing. "That's number one, by a mile. Then number two is I listened to classical piano music online yesterday because of Andrew."

His whole face lit up. "Did you really?"

"Yep. Though maybe it's not number two. Maybe it's number three and the smiling like an idiot is number two. The polls are pretty close."

He was just beaming. "You're so funny."

"Now, if you don't mind, I need to go check out this bookstore, and while waiting to see if psycho Lance turns up, I need to do something totally romantic like buy a book that I know my boyfriend would like."

Andrew was still smiling. "Oh yeah, like what?"

"Like *How to Have Sex With Your Boyfriend When He's Hung Like a Horse*," I joked. "Oh wait, no that one's for me. For you, I'd probably buy *How to Abstain From Sex Without Dying.*"

He busted up laughing. "Is that so?"

"Yep, it's a best-seller."

"There is never a dull moment with you, is there?"

"I hope not."

He looked at me for a long moment, like he wanted to say something but couldn't. Instead, he squeezed my hand and led me toward the bookstore. "Come on. Let's go see if we can find you that book."

"The one about my boyfriend being hung like a horse?"

He chuckled. "Yep. I somehow think we'll find it next to the one titled *101 Uses For Lube*."

I loved that he played along. "Excellent. Hopefully there's free samples."

He groaned. "We really shouldn't be talking about this in public."

"Why not?" I looked around at the people walking past. "It's not like anyone gives a crap."

"No. Talking about—" He side-eyed me as he walked. "—*that* with you is giving me that problem I had earlier."

I laughed. Jesus. He was relentless. "Shall we find the bathrooms first?"

He growled at me and mumbled something that sounded like "Don't tempt me," but dragged me into the bookstore.

He didn't go to the bathrooms but went past the coffee shop inside the bookstore and headed straight for the escalator to the second floor. "Where are we going?"

"Upstairs," he answered. "Would it not be a better vantage point to see if whatshisname comes in?"

"Well, true," I conceded. "Though I'm a little disappointed you're not taking me to the bathrooms."

He looked over his shoulder and glared at me. "How are we supposed to make it till Saturday if you keep being suggestive like that?"

I laughed quietly, ignoring the ache in my balls at all the talk of sex with him.

"It's not funny, Spencer," he said. "Maybe I should just fuck you tonight."

I tripped up the last step of the escalator. "Jesus, Andrew."

Now it was his turn to laugh as he led me to the first stack of books near the balcony. "Not so funny when the shoe's on the other foot, is it?"

"Caught me off guard, that's all," I said, pretending he didn't shock the hell out of me. "And anyway, it wasn't strictly an unpleasant visual image."

Andrew took a deep breath and changed subjects. "So, what does this guy look like?"

"Like a slimy creep. I'll take a guess that he'll have just left work, so he'll be here in about twenty minutes I'd say, wearing an expensive suit and a cheap smile." I looked down at the entrance to the bookstore but couldn't see anyone that even looked remotely like him. I put my hand on Andrew's arm. "I don't want him to see me with you."

Andrew's gaze shot to mine, instant offence and rejection in his eyes. "Why not?"

I smiled softly at him. "No other reason than I just don't want you implicated in this in anyway. If he is the arsehole I assume he is, I don't want him to even look at you. I don't want him anywhere near you."

"Oh."

"Do you think I would not want the world to know we're together?" I asked. "If you want me to broadcast an ad on CBS, I will."

He smiled now, the corner of his mouth lifted shyly. "Thanks, but that's not necessary."

"No?"

He shook his head. "An ad in the *LA Times* would be fine."

I snorted. "Is that all?"

He nodded. "Or a whole page ad in *Sexy Geek*. I hear their running a special edition titled *How to Keep your Sexy Geek Satisfied*."

I couldn't help but grin. "Really? I should definitely buy that."

"You should subscribe," he said, like it was a matter of fact. "Now, given we're incognito, I'm going back downstairs to have a coffee, see if I can pick up some random hottie."

My mouth fell open, and a pang of hurt bloomed in my heart. How did we go from joking to him wanting someone else? "What?"

He quickly took my hand and squeezed it. "I was only joking!"

"Oh."

I think my reaction secretly pleased him. "But, later, if whathisname doesn't turn up, I'll be hanging around pretending not to know you, and if you're, you know, not too busy, you can try your best pick-up lines on me." His whole face softened. "You're my random hottie, Spencer."

My heart tripped all over itself. "Oh. Well, that's all right then. Because if there was a magazine called *The Only Guy Spencer Wants*, you'd be on the cover."

He smiled so perfectly. So happy and smug and shy, all rolled into one.

I looked around for the closest bathroom to drag him into, because seriously, I wanted him. I didn't just want him in my bed, I wanted him in my life. For the next however long. Forever, probably. And *that* realisation—the forever kind of realisation—rattled me. I had known this guy for just a few weeks, but he was perfect for me. Not a perfect person, because no one was, but perfect *for me*. The yin to my yang, the piece to my puzzle, the jazz and classical to my rock and blues. We were compatible on an intellectual level, and physically... well, I could only imagine what it was going to be like when we finally started having actual fuck sessions. I was pretty sure we'd never stop. And the word forever didn't just drift through my mind like an errant thought. It stomped.

Me, the guy who purposely kept people at arm's length, was thinking of relationships of the permanent variety. Maybe it was the absurd butterflies in my stomach that made my ludicrous endorphins mess with the synapses in my stupid brain.

"You okay?" Andrew asked, concern written all over his face.

"I am super great," I answered, ignoring the butterflies trying to escape through my chest.

"Super great? Is that a thing?"

"Yes." According to my stupid brain, it's very much a thing. "Yes it is."

He laughed. "Okay, then. I'm going to grab a coffee," he said, leaving me on the second floor with my brain still stuck on that one word. Forever. And those bloody butterflies that turned my stomach into a roiling mess made my feet stick to the floor and plastered a ridiculous grin on my face, and I wasn't sure if I wanted to holler from the rooftops as to how happy I was. Or vomit.

It wasn't until some guy looked at me like I was some sort of creeper that I made myself move. I stood at the shelves of books with a view of the front door, but also of the tables and chairs of the coffee shop inside the store. Andrew ordered and took a seat, kind of looking at the entrance, but I could still see his face. He was wearing a smile similar to mine, I'd imagine. It was an unstoppable smile, a can't-help-it smile, a he-must-feel-the-same-way smile.

I was just about to pull the pin on this foolish covert operation and drag Andrew out of here. I fully intended to forgo the jazz bar and just take him home and take him to bed. But figured I should at least pretend to look over some books to buy for Andrew. I was in the crime section as it turned out, and that wasn't really my genre of choice. With one eye on the doors and one eye on the shelves, and an occasional glance at a still-smiling Andrew, I took out my phone and shot him a text.

> You're really hot, you know that?

I watched as he pulled out his phone. His grin was instantaneous. He thumbed the screen for a second, and my phone buzzed straight after.

> Is that your best pick up line? Because it needs work.

I laughed quietly at my screen and quickly typed back my response.

> Oh, I can do much better than that...

But then I noticed a guy walk into the store who looked familiar, and when I looked again, I could see it was Lance.

He scoured the floor first, kind of slinking off to the side. Then he was underneath the second floor where I was standing, and I lost visual contact. I sent a quick text to Andrew before I pocketed my phone

> He's here.

I worried for a moment that Andrew might look up and around the store very obviously, but he was very stealthy. For a sexy geek, that is. He still smiled at his phone but his eyes looked around the room, before he put his phone down, sipped his coffee, and picked up a magazine.

I took the escalator back to the ground floor and went in the direction I'd seen Lance the Tosser go. I found him standing at the back, almost hiding behind a row of shelves, trying to be inconspicuous as he scanned the room. I walked directly up to him, and he did a double take when he saw me.

"Great minds think alike, huh?" I said, offering him my hand to shake.

He shook it but was clearly uncomfortable. "Spencer? What are you doing here?"

"What you're paying me to do," I replied quietly. No one else needed to hear this conversation. "Follow leads, and hopefully find Yanni. I could possibly ask you the same thing."

"Well, you mentioned he worked here," he said. He even had the gall to look all sheepish about it. Then he sighed and frowned, his forehead creased with worry. "I just want to see him."

Man, he was good. I wondered, very briefly, if I had him pegged wrong. Could he have been honestly concerned for Yanni and I read him all wrong? Was I way off the mark on the whole situation? I had to admit, now I wasn't sure. But in keeping with the lies I'd told him about Yanni working here, I said, "He's not here. I've asked already."

"But he does work here?"

"I spoke to a girl working upstairs. She said she hadn't worked here long, but there was no Yanni here today, and the staff here now are the only ones working until closing time.

That was all she said. He could be rostered on tomorrow or next week or not at all. I don't know."

Lance sighed, and slowly started to nod. "Okay."

I looked out the glass wall at the front, using the opportunity to also see if Andrew was sitting at the café. He was, thankfully. "It's dark out. You just finished work?"

"Yeah," he mumbled. "I should probably get going home."

"Oh, sure thing," I said.

Lance took a step away, then stopped. "Is this the lead you were talking about? You said there was one more lead in looking for him."

"Oh, yeah. It is. Well, it was," I amended quickly. "I can make some more calls tomorrow if you like."

He looked to the floor, then back to me. "I dunno... I guess he's just gone."

Shit. Either this guy was genuine, or he deserved an Oscar. "Look, I'll see what I can find tomorrow, and I'll be in touch. Don't make any decisions right now."

He nodded, forced a smile, and left. I watched him go, and when he'd disappeared into the night, I looked at Andrew.

He was still sitting there, but he was now looking at me, his expression curious and a little concerned.

I gave him a smile and remembered the little game he wanted to play. I held up my finger in a 'one-second' gesture and disappeared around the stacks of books. I needed to find the perfect thing... It took a little more than one second, but after I found it. Actually, I found two.

Holding one of the books behind my back so he couldn't see it, I walked over. I stood at the chair in front of him. "Excuse me, would you mind if I sat down?"

He smiled but played along. "Please do."

I sat on the seat, letting the book behind my back stay out of view. "Can I ask you a question?"

"Sure."

"Do you ever wonder why the most common gestures of affection are to give flowers or chocolates?"

Andrew snorted quietly. "It's not something I've given a great deal of thought to, no."

"I have."

"Is that right?" he said, trying to be serious. He slid the magazine back onto the table. "And what conclusion did you come to?"

I sighed. "Well, it's a good gesture. A nice thing to do, really. If the person you wish to impress likes flowers and chocolates. But it's become very impersonal. Like the person has put no thought into what would make the intended recipient happy. I think it's an antiquated gesture, when life was simpler."

He nodded thoughtfully. "A simpler life is not overrated."

"True," I conceded. "But if it were me, I'd like to think I knew what to get the person. A gift that would mean something. Something more personal than flowers."

Andrew was clearly delighted. He eyed the upturned book in my lap, trying to read the title. "Is that so? Pray tell, if you were to give someone a gift—someone such as myself—what do you think you would choose?"

"Ah, see there's the crux of my dilemma. If I could choose, I would pick you a vinyl album."

"Or a whole record player..."

"Yes well, that too. But I would choose you a Jeff Buckley album, or a Bill Withers record."

Andrew laughed. "But this is not a vintage LP store."

"How very astute! Right you are! Which is why I chose this book for you." I handed him the first book.

He read the title out loud. "*A Geek's Guide to Cooking.*" He looked from the book to my face. He tilted his head and narrowed his eyes, absolutely thrown by my choice. "Really? Is this meant to flatter, insult, or amuse?"

I was trying not to laugh. "All three, of course."

"Well, two out of three isn't bad." He flipped through the pages. "And this is your very serious attempt at picking me up?"

I shook my head slowly and produced the other book from behind my back. I held it so he could only see the back, and my heart was beating double time. I hoped to hell I got this right. "This book is."

Very nervously, I handed it over.

He read the title, and his gaze shot to mine. His smile was slow spreading, his eyes warm and shining. He whispered, "Spencer... it's perfect."

I let out a relieved laugh. "Really?"

He nodded, and absentmindedly reread the title. "*Do Androids Dream of Electric Sheep?* This is an absolute classic, Spencer. Blade Runner was based off this book."

"I know, that's why I chose it for you."

He stared at me, then back at the book in his hands, as though his emotions got the better of him. "You know me..." He shook his head, seemingly unable to finish.

I tapped his foot with mine and waited for him to look up. "And you know me."

He stared at me. Just stared. And eventually he swallowed hard and let out a long steadying breath. "Can we leave?"

I nodded and stood up. I held my hand out to him, which he took, and let me pull him to his feet. "I have to pay for the books first," I told him. Then it got the better of me. "So, did I pass?"

"Pass what?"

"The pickup line test."

Andrew chuckled. "You really did."

I grinned at him and spoke so only he could hear. "Am I gonna get lucky tonight?"

He blushed. "Let me think… you're buying me one of the coolest books ever written and taking me to a jazz bar. I think it's safe to assume there will be luck involved when we get home."

"How lucky?" I whispered. "Because I know we said we'd wait until this weekend, but a guy can live in hope, right?"

Andrew smiled salaciously. "That totally depends on whether you feed me as well."

"Oh, I see how it is," I joked. "You expect books, jazz music, *and* dinner."

He sniffed. "I do have standards."

I laughed and took his hand, leading him to the service counter. Andrew looked at the cookbook. "You're seriously buying me the cooking for geeks book?"

"Absolutely. I've made it my mission in life to teach you how to cook."

He scowled at me, but he hardly meant it. It was more smile than scowl. "I'm only cooking if you're there to help me."

"Deal." I paid for the books, and when the cashier handed me the bag with the books in it, I turned to face Andrew. I took a deep breath and slowly held them out for him, like I would if they were flowers. "For you."

I expected some snarky comment or at least an eye roll, but he blushed a little and smiled all shy-like. He took the books graciously. "Thank you."

I wanted to kiss him. I wanted to slide my hand along his jaw to his neck so much my palm tingled. But I didn't. The bookstore was crowded, and we'd not really discussed PDAs outside of a darkened bar. Hand-holding was one thing, kissing another.

"We should go," I said; my voice was gruff. I cleared my throat. "The bar's not far from here apparently."

Andrew licked his lips as though he wanted to kiss me just as much as I wanted him to, but instead he stared at me for a long second before nodding. "Yeah. We should."

I led the way to the doors, kicking myself that I'd promised him we'd go to a jazz bar. Going back to his place and taking him to bed seemed like such a better idea. But, like a good boy, instead of hailing a cab and going home, I pointed up the street. "This way."

TEN

THE AIR OUTSIDE WAS LIKE A MAGIC ANTIDOTE TO THE
sexual tension between us. My need to take him into a dark
alley and push him against a wall, slipping in between his
thighs and kissing him until he surrendered seemed to dissi-
pate into the LA night above us. But it was never far away,
just under the surface, itching to pick up where we left off,
waiting for the perfect moment to take him home.

We grabbed a quick bite to eat on the way, too keen to
check out the jazz scene. As we neared the bar, we had to run
across the street, and Andrew took my hand, only letting it go
when we got to the door. Inside the bar was dark and not
overly crowded, but enough to afford perfect anonymity and
getting cosy in the corner. It reminded me of a bohemian
poet's hangout, shabby chic but elegant enough to explain the
ridiculously priced drinks.

I told Andrew to grab a table while I went to the bar, and
while I waited, I noticed the stage. It was centred along the
far wall, and on the stage was an old piano, a double bass
stood in its stand, and a clarinet and trombone stood upright
in their stands. It looked kind of sad and lonely, seeing these

instruments without their musicians, but when I glanced over at Andrew, he was sitting at a table looking at the stage as well. And he was just beaming.

How on earth his ex had never taken him to a jazz bar, I'll never know. I'd bring him to one every day of the week if I could, just to see him smile like that.

The barman interrupted my musings, so I ordered two beers and finally fell into a seat next to Andrew. I handed him the beer and pressed my knee and thigh against his. "Looks good," I said, nodding toward the stage.

He agreed, still grinning. "Yeah." He took a swig from his bottle. "So, Lance turned up like you thought he would. What did he have to say?"

I swallowed my mouthful of beer. "He said he just wants to see him. Everything he says, how he reacts, it's either all genuine or he's a very good actor."

"What do you think?"

I shrugged. "I don't know what to make of it. Of *him*. I want to believe him, but there's something about him I can't put my finger on."

Andrew sipped his beer and nodded. "Well, you know what they say about your sixth sense?"

"I see dead people?"

He laughed. "No. That you get that feeling for a reason. There's a reason the hairs on the back of your neck stand on end. That creepy feeling to warn you of danger, it's a real thing."

"You believe that?"

He looked me right in the eye. "Yes I do."

"Do you believe in fate?"

His eyes flashed with something—amusement, daring, honesty?—and he took a second to answer. "I never used to. I'm more of a logical, scientific reasoning kind of guy."

I sipped my beer to hide my smile. "You used past tense, so never used to, but you do now?"

"The jury's still out. I'm undecided."

"It's not difficult. You either do or you don't?"

"Do you?"

"Yes."

"You think it's fate that things happen for a reason?"

"I think we choose our own paths, make our own decisions, but I think the people who come into your life do so for good reason."

"So, your decision to come to America?"

"Completely my decision, but I was destined to be here."

"That doesn't make sense," he argued. "You can't have both."

"Says who?"

He frowned, flustered. "Well, the rules of destiny."

"The rules of destiny?"

He barked out a laugh. "Shut up."

"Is that even a thing?"

"Well, yes! I just made it a thing."

"So our lives, our entire existence, is like some cosmic board game, where our makers roll a dice and move our little markers all over the board?"

He laughed again. "Yep, exactly," he said, rolling his eyes. "Like The Game of Life, but only for real."

"Well, I'd personally like to sincerely thank my maker for rolling whatever number led you to me," I told him. I never took my eyes off him as I had another drink of beer. "I certainly landed on Mayfair when I met you."

"May, what?"

"Mayfair. You know, the dark blue, most expensive street on Monopoly?"

He laughed. "You mean Boardwalk. Anyway, which is totally not The Game of Life, but okay."

Just then, some guys took to the stage and sat on stools at their chosen instruments. Any chance of conversation between us was lost because Andrew turned his full attention to them. Well, almost full. He turned his chair a little so he was facing them better and slid his hand onto my thigh under the table and looked as happy and intrigued as I'd seen him.

The band was good, and they played a bunch of songs Andrew was familiar with. He seemed genuinely impressed. Not that I was any expert, but I leaned in and whispered, my lips at his ear, "You can play the piano better than him."

Andrew chuckled. "Uh, probably not."

I leaned back in. "Uh, probably yes."

He shook his head, dismissing me altogether. "I think you're biased."

"I think you're sexy."

He laughed, his warm breath rushed over my neck, and I was just about to pull back and kiss him when the music stopped. They announced a short break, and the room filled with chatter and recorded background music, which paled in comparison to what we'd just heard. "You should go play the piano while they're having a break," I told him.

"What?" he said, alarmed. "No way!"

"Yes way. Give these good people a lesson in music."

He shook his head. "You don't just play someone else's instrument, Spencer."

"Is that like some cardinal sin?"

"Absolutely."

"What if you asked first?" I looked around to see if I could see the guy who'd been playing the piano, but he wasn't anywhere I could see.

Andrew grabbed my arm. "No, no. Don't even think about

it." He looked at his watch. "Come on, it's getting late, and I have to work in the morning."

"They still have to play another set," I tried to reason, looking toward the stage, but Andrew stood up.

He picked up the books I'd bought him. "Is it okay if we go early? I've had the best night, but it's almost eleven."

"Sure," I said, standing with him. "I didn't mean to scare you off. I wouldn't have asked without your permission."

He gave me a tight smile. "No, it's not that..."

I could tell it totally was. "Well, we better get you home before the stroke of midnight."

"I won't turn into a pumpkin," he mumbled.

"Shame. I love eating pumpkin."

He laughed again; the smile that lingered was genuine.

We hailed a cab and climbed into the back. Andrew gave directions to his place, sat right up close to me, and held my hand. "I did have the best night," he said, not caring if the cabbie heard or saw us. "But I figured it'll take us a while to get home, then to fall asleep..." He blushed.

Mmm, the mere hint of suggestiveness made my whole body warm. "Oh, any particular plans I should know about?"

"I thought we could improvise," he said.

"I like improvising."

He sighed and leaned against me. Traffic was fairly steady, and we had a decent fifteen minute cab ride ahead of us. I couldn't blame him for getting comfortable. I put my arm around his shoulder, and he sighed contentedly. "Can I ask you something?"

"Sure," I answered, hoping it was a question laced with innuendo. Mental foreplay was a lot of fun. "But before you ask, no I've never played naked Twister before."

He snorted. "That totally wasn't my question."

"Shame."

"It's about your family."

I blinked, shocked. I wasn't expecting that at all. "Oh."

He sat up. "No, sorry, it's nothing. I shouldn't have said anything."

I wasn't sure what he could possibly want to know. I hadn't mentioned them since that first day we really got together, after my complete meltdown when I thought Andrew had gone back to his ex. I also hadn't thought of them since then. I'd been too busy—too happy—with Andrew. "It's okay," I said, swallowing thickly. "Ask away."

"No, it was silly, and I shouldn't have mentioned them."

"Well, you have now, so just ask."

He furrowed his brow and the corner of his lip pulled down. "It was just about fate and destiny, that's all. You said you believed everything happened for a reason..." He shrugged. "Just forget I mentioned them. Sorry."

"You're wondering if I believe that all things happen for a reason, what purpose my family disowning me could possibly mean?"

He frowned and pulled back, putting a distance between us. "I'm sorry."

"Andrew, would you stop apologising?"

He shook his head. "I do this, you know. Ruin things, that is. I say things that affront people, and I ruin things."

"You didn't ruin anything."

He rolled his eyes, and I really couldn't tell if it was aimed at me, or at himself. He was certainly pissed with himself. His jaw clenched and he stared out the window, like he couldn't bear to look at me. And just like that, he shut me out. I knew I was new to relationships, in the whole scheme of things, and somewhat defensive by nature. But this reaction from him threw me completely. I had no idea how we went from having the best night, to a silent void between us.

"Andrew, would you look at me?"

He did and waited for me to speak.

"You didn't ruin anything by asking me a question."

"It was insensitive, and I should have known better."

"I'm not made of glass," I told him, pissed off he thought I was *that* fragile. "I know I have… issues when it comes to my family. The meltdown I had when we first met was a combination of things, and I'm sorry you got caught up in that, but it doesn't mean you have to walk on eggshells around me. If you want to fucking know something, then ask."

He blinked, shocked. "You're angry," he whispered. "See? This is what I do."

"I'm not angry that you asked me about my family, Andrew. I'm angry that you think you have to censor yourself around me, and when I question that, your first reaction is to put a wall up between us."

He swallowed hard. "I'm sorry."

"Please stop apologising."

"But I am. I ruined the perfect night."

"You didn't ruin it."

"Well, you're angry with me so I'd consider that ruined."

I put my hands through my hair and realised the cab had turned into Andrew's street. "I'm not angry," I said softly.

"You just said you were," he countered.

The cab stopped and I sighed, defeated. Did I get out with him? Did he even want me to? He put his hand on the door handle. "You should probably just go home," he said.

Right, then. No guessing required.

He opened the door, and I grabbed his arm. "Andrew, what just happened?"

He smiled ruefully. "I told you. I ruined it." He passed some money to the cab driver and got out. He turned to face me, and the look on his face squeezed my heart. "I'll call you," he choked out and closed the door.

And I sat there, my head spinning, with no clue what the fuck just happened.

"Where to?" the cabbie asked.

I looked at the driver's eyes in the rear vision mirror. And every book and every movie that I hated, where the characters bickered over something stupid and miscommunication and pride fucked everything up, ran through my head. I hated that they wouldn't just grow the fuck up and talk to each other. It was cliché, it was immature, and I understood now that it was very fucking real.

I still hated it.

I pulled out my wallet and threw a tenner to the cabbie for making him wait. "Right here, mate," I said, getting out. I slammed the door and stomped after Andrew.

He'd just got his key in the door and opened it. "What are you doing?" he asked.

I grabbed his hand and pulled him inside. "We're going to fucking talk."

His place was dark, save the hall light that cast a faint light out into his living room. He was still holding the books I'd bought him like they were some defensive shield, so I took them from him and threw them onto the sofa. He looked at the floor between us, and Jesus, he looked like he was about to cry.

So I did the only thing I could think of doing. I pulled him against me. I wrapped my arms around him, and he held me just as tight. It felt so good. It was true: hugs had healing powers. He fit against me just right, not in a sexual way, but in a fixing kind of way. I could feel the tenseness leave his shoulders, and after a moment he relaxed into me.

He mumbled against my shirt, "I don't know what happened."

I pulled back just a little and lifted his chin so I could kiss him. It was a soft kiss, an emotional kiss. "Please don't ever not talk to me," I whispered. "Don't cut me off, don't ignore me. It's the one thing..." I swallowed hard. "It's what they did."

His eyes widened before slowly closing. He knew I was talking about my family. "God, Spencer, I'm sorry."

"Be mad, be upset, but please don't walk away from me."

He took my face in his hands and kissed me before bringing my face into his neck. He held me so tight. "I didn't realise," he said. "I really fucked up."

"No you didn't," I mumbled into his neck. "We're learning as we go, that's all."

"Thank you," he whispered, pressing his lips to the side of my head. "Thank you for not going home. Thank you for making me listen."

I pulled back then and cupped his face, tracing his jaw with my thumbs. "You just shut down on me."

"I know. I don't mean to. It was just the most perfect night —I had the best night, I really did—and I wanted to bring you back here and take you to bed. I thought tonight might be the night, ya know? But then I say the most senseless things when I get nervous. I have no filter, and I'm socially awkward. I always have been. It's painful, seriously. I wish I knew how to not ruin things."

I kissed his eyelids, his cheek, then his lips. "You didn't ruin anything."

He snorted. "Okay."

"I'm still here, aren't I?"

He stared at me then. "Yes. Thank God you got out of that cab."

"It always bothers me in movies with miscommunication as the trope. It's so cliché. And out of all the things, Andrew, we're not cliché. We're not *When Harry Met Sally*. We're more like the movie *Seven*. With the head in the box."

He blinked. "*Seven*?"

"Well, okay. Not in the psychopathic-murdering-madmen kind of way but in the unexpected kind of way. Nobody expected the head in the box."

He finally laughed. "No mutilated heads in a box, and no walking away."

"No."

He breathed in deeply and leaned into my hand. "I don't want to have sex."

A bubble of laughter escaped me. "Oh, okay."

He straightened, alarmed. "No, no, I didn't mean it like that. Oh God, I've done it again. I meant tonight. I just meant it wouldn't be right *tonight*. I want it to be when it won't feel like a pity fuck."

Now I laughed, long and loud. "Oh Andrew—" I kissed him. "—you are one of a kind."

His shoulders sagged, and he wouldn't look at me. "Will you stay anyway?"

I lifted his face so he could see I was smiling. I kissed him again. "I will stay. No sex though. But I want to wake up next to you, is that okay?"

He nodded. "Very."

"And you will never be a pity fuck."

"I say the most stupidest things."

"And I have a stupid brain, so we make a good pair."

"At least your stupid brain has a filter." He blinked. "I didn't mean you actually had a stupid brain."

I snorted. "How about we just call it a day?"

He nodded slowly. "That's probably a good idea."

Taking his hand, I led him up the stairs and into his room. We didn't bother with showers or brushing our teeth, we simply stripped to our underwear and got into bed. He slid over to me and put his head on my chest, my arms instinctively wrapped around him. His breaths were steady but I could feel his eyelashes every time he blinked. After a long silence, I said, "Can I answer your question?"

He waited.

"I believe in fate. I believe there was good reason my family, my parents mostly, disowned me. I got to spend some great years with my Aunt Marvie, who was the kindest woman I'd ever met. I'd like to think I made the last few years of her life happy ones. Yes, she gave me money, but I'd give it all back for one more day with her. I came here to LA, I met Lola and Emilio, and they're the best friends a guy could ask for. And I met you." My heart was just about to burst, but I had to say this. "This is the life I was supposed to live. Here, right now, in your bed with you."

Andrew leaned up and looked me right in the eyes. "Spencer," he whispered. He put his hand to my face and kissed me, soft and warm, with a gentle swipe of his tongue. When he pulled his mouth from mine, he rested his forehead on my cheek and fell back against me.

I rolled onto my side a little, keeping him right where he was, his face firmly planted in the crook of my neck, and we fell asleep wrapped in each other's arms.

ELEVEN

I woke up when Andrew got out of bed. "Mm mm," I grumbled. "Come back." I must have been spooning him, because I missed the warmth down my entire front when he was gone.

He chuckled. "Some of us have to work," he said, as he walked toward his bathroom.

"I work," I objected, sleepily. "Kind of."

I heard the shower start a moment later and rolled onto my back. His bed really was the most comfortable bed in the world. My hand naturally went to my dick to give my morning wood a squeeze. One thing I knew for certain, my body liked waking up spooning Andrew.

My heart didn't mind it either.

Despite how the night took a nosedive, I was pretty sure we'd be okay.

And then my sleep addled brain caught up...

Andrew was naked in the next room, wet and soapy...

I got out of bed, and seeing he'd left the door ajar, I knocked before cautiously walking in. "Any objections to company?"

He had a headful of shampoo, but that's not where my eyes were drawn. His dick was full and hanging heavily. I swallowed hard, and my cock filled at the sight of him. He laughed at me. "No objections at all. But I have to leave in twenty minutes. I already missed the gym."

I pulled my underpants off, freeing my eager and already-leaking erection. "Really?"

"Yes, I woke up in time, but there was a hot guy in my bed with his arms around me and his beard pressed against the back of my ear."

I stepped into the shower, and he never took his eyes from mine. His self-control really was rather impressive. I scratched my beard. "You like it?"

"I love it," he whispered.

I stood in front of him. Steam filled the space between us, and I remembered what he said. "Twenty minutes, huh?"

He could either read minds or there was something in my tone because he smiled. "Before I have to leave. Not twenty minutes shower time."

I dropped to my knees. "I won't be long."

He groaned even before I'd taken him into my mouth. His fingers gripped my hair and he guided me to how he liked it. Which was deep and thoroughly, apparently. I never really had him pegged as the skull-fucking type, but he was right into it, and in just a few minutes, he came down my throat. He pulled out of my mouth and yanked my head back by my hair, only to plant his mouth on mine. Then he lifted me to my feet and went to his knees where he returned the favour. I'd like to think I lasted longer than him, but I doubt I did. He left me slumped against the tiles, happily seeing stars in the steam, and incapable of coherent thought.

Then he shut the water off and threw a towel at me with a laugh. "You alive in there?"

"Mmm, barely." I dried myself off and put the towel over my head, drying my hair in a sawing motion, leaving it sticking up in every direction.

Andrew was at the basin, towel around his waist, brushing his teeth, and he chuckled at me. "That's a good look," he mumbled around his toothbrush.

I swung my towel over my shoulder, leaving myself naked beside him, and stole his hair comb from the counter. I combed my hair flat against my head, parted at the side, in a very not-like-me hairdo. When Andrew finished brushing his teeth and saw it, he burst out laughing. "Mm-mm," he hummed disapprovingly. Then he ran his fingers through my hair and took the comb, styling it to how he liked it apparently.

When I checked the mirror, he'd done it exactly how I normally wore it. It was shaved on the sides, long on top, and he'd made a quiff. Without a word, he started to foam his face with shaving cream, and I watched, transfixed, as he shaved. Stroke by meticulous stroke, he rid his face of white foam and scruff, carefully lifting and turning his face for the best angles.

I was surprised at how much I liked to watch him do this.

I surveyed my beard in the mirror. "Mmm, maybe I should shave."

Andrew rinsed off his face and patted it dry with the towel off my shoulder. He shook his head. "Don't change a thing."

"You like my beard, don't you?"

He smiled, almost shyly. "I do. I never thought about guys with beards before I met you, but I do, yes."

I surveyed myself in the mirror again. "I do need to trim it though."

"Trim is fine; don't shave it."

I smiled at his tone. "Sounds like an order."

When I turned around, he was staring at my naked arse. When he realised I'd caught him ogling, he shrugged unapologetically. "I could get used to this view every morning."

I nodded toward the shower. "I could get used to bathroom blowjobs every morning."

He laughed as he walked out into his walk-through robe. "Those too."

"Hey, can I borrow some toothpaste?" I asked.

"Sure, but I certainly don't want it back." He stopped, just short of removing the towel from his waist. He frowned. "I still don't have a spare toothbrush. I thought I did, but I don't."

"I thought we decided it was too soon for toothbrushes anyway," I said, half joking, half not. I held up my finger. "This'll do till I get home." I squirted some toothpaste onto my index finger and crudely brushed over my teeth with it. I rinsed and spat into the sink. "Better than furry teeth."

"True," Andrew said. He'd already donned some undies, but I had the immense pleasure of watching him pull on blue trousers and a white business shirt. As he was buttoning the shirt, he smiled at me. "You just gonna watch?"

"Yep."

"Not gonna get dressed?"

I was still naked. "Only if I have to."

"I'm not opposed—" He raked his eyes up and down my body. "—at all. But the general public might not appreciate the view."

I had no clean clothes to wear, so with a shrug, I raided his wardrobe. I found some older black trousers, of which I rolled the cuffs up so they looked like they fit me. "You'll have to think of me going commando all day," I told him. He groaned, and I smiled as I plucked a pink T-shirt from the bottom of his pile of neatly folded shirts.

"I've never worn that shirt," he said. "My mom bought it for me last year." He looked me up and down. "How do you make those clothes look so good? I would never have worn them together."

I pulled one of his grey knitted vests from a hanger and handed it to him. "With these pants?" He looked at me like I'd lost my mind.

"Yep."

He mumbled something I couldn't quite make out but pulled the vest over his head anyway. I nodded approvingly and turned him around so he could see himself in his mirror. "Oh, that's not bad."

"Not bad? That's fucking hot." I put one hand around his neck and pulled him in for a kiss. I ran my other hand over his arse and pulled him against me, lifting his leg around my hip, and plunged my tongue into his mouth.

When I was done kissing him, he stood there, stunned, somewhat violated and very kiss-drunk. He smiled lazily. "Wow."

I laughed at him. "Now you can think about that all day too."

He slowly adjusted himself. "Thanks."

"You're very welcome." I collected my pile of clothes from his bedroom floor. "Come on, or you'll be late for work."

He looked at the rumpled bed, then back to me and licked his lips. "I'm considering calling in sick."

I laughed at him. "No you're not. I won't be held account-able for your lack of productivity."

He walked past me to the door. "If we stayed here, we could be very productive."

Now it was me who had to adjust himself, which thankfully he didn't see. I'm pretty sure if he did, we wouldn't be leaving his house any time soon. When I got down the stairs behind him, he was sitting on the sofa pulling on his socks and shoes, and when he was done, he picked up the paper bag he'd thrown there last night.

He slid the books out I'd bought him and sighed. "Thank you again, for buying me these. Well," he amended, "the cooking one not so much, but this one... this one I love." He stared at the *Do Androids Dream of Electric Sheep?* book I'd picked for him. He looked up at me then. "And thank you for not going home last night, for not giving up on me."

"You're welcome."

He stood up and walked over to stand right in front of me. He looked me in the eye and said, "I promise I'll talk to you. I won't shut you out."

It was different to hear your insecurities in the light of day. I didn't know why, but talking of such things in darkened rooms seemed so much easier. I was a little embarrassed when he brought it up now. I guessed that was the irony of my request for open communication. "Thanks."

"I really wish I didn't have to go to work today," he whispered.

"Me too," I answered honestly. "But I told Emilio I'd help him out this morning, and Lola's taking me to some college in a last ditch effort to find this Yanni guy this arvo."

He squinted at me. "What's an arvo?"

"Afternoon. This arvo is Australian for this afternoon."

"Oh."

"But it's more one word, like thisarvo."

He laughed and grabbed his keys and wallet. He opened the front door. "Tell me, do Australians really say *crikey*?"

I walked past him. "No. As a general rule. Not ever."

We walked to his car. "What about *g'day mate* instead of hello?"

"All the time. But usually just *g'day* or *mate*. We might say *g'day, how're ya goin'?* or *hey mate*. Generally not *g'day mate* together. Sometimes but not always, unless you're taking the piss."

"So you need to have a lobotomy to be Australian?"

I stared at him over the roof of his car. "I am truly offended."

He laughed. "No you're not."

He climbed into the driver's seat, and I got into the passenger's side. "I am offended, I'll have you know. Just as I'm offended that you didn't serve me green tea this morning."

He drove the car out onto the street but eyed me cautiously. "I could buy some."

I sniffed. "And breakfast? Where was that?"

"Um, well it was late, and I already missed the gym."

"I mean, the protein shake I had in your shower was good and all, but not enough to keep me going."

He barked out a laugh, and his cheeks tinted pink. "Oh my God, Spencer."

"Does that embarrass you?"

He glared at me as he drove and tried to not smile but failed. "A little, yes."

"And now you're thinking about what we did in the shower, aren't you?"

"I wasn't," he said. He shifted in his seat. "But now I am."

"And now you're thinking about me being commando, aren't you?"

He shot me a glare but looked back to the road and swallowed hard. "No."

"You totally are."

He squirmed in his seat. "I hate you."

I grinned at him. "No you don't." I took his free hand and kissed the back of it. "I'm sorry."

"You're really not."

"No, I'm not really." We were both smiling, and I kept hold of his hand on my thigh. "But I promise to talk about something else for the remainder of the drive."

"I should have made you catch the bus." He squeezed my hand. "But perhaps a change of topic in conversation would be a good idea."

I sighed. "What are you doing tonight?"

"Well, I was going to go see my boyfriend, but he's being a bit of a jerk. I'm sure he wants me to go to work with a semi."

I cracked up laughing. "Still thinking about me being commando?"

He groaned. "I hate you."

"No you don't."

He laughed. "No, I don't. But I was thinking I'll probably go to the gym tonight. Can we do something tomorrow night?"

"For sure. Oh, I'm buying dinner for everyone tomorrow night as a thanks for helping me out when this hot guy I really liked was gonna do a runner." I shook my head. "God, was that only a week ago?"

He squeezed my hand. "I know. Pretty hard to believe, huh? And for the record, I was never gonna do a runner."

I kissed his knuckles again before putting his hand back on my thigh. "But then this weekend you're all mine, so don't go making any plans."

His smile was smug. "I'm all yours, am I?"

I could see Emilio's shop up ahead so I knew I didn't have much time. "Yes you are. We said we'd make it to this weekend before we take turns fucking each other's brains out, remember?"

Andrew's eyes widened and he blushed. "Right."

"I thought you could fuck me all day Saturday, then on Sunday it's my turn to have you."

His breath was all pitchy, and he struggled to change lanes. Without saying a word, he stopped in front of Emilio's, and I pushed his hand on my thickening dick and whispered, "Just thinking about it…" I groaned. "I'm gonna have to go upstairs and take care of this."

He made a whining noise in the back of his throat and squirmed. He pulled back his hand. "I hate you."

I laughed as I leaned over and kissed his cheek. "No you don't." I got out of the car and watched him drive off and was still chuckling as I walked into the tattoo shop.

"Hey, you're looking far too happy for this time of day, my friend," Emilio said.

"Gimme ten minutes to drop these dirty clothes off," I told him, holding up my bundle of yesterday's clothes. "Then I'll do a breakfast run. How does that sound?"

"Sounds great," he said.

I went through the back of the shop and up to my flat above it. It wasn't just to drop off laundry. I wasn't kidding when I told Andrew I'd have to take care of myself, and it took all of two minutes to bring myself to climax despite already coming once that morning. Just thinking about sex with him did me in. When I was cleaned up and clear-headed, I sent Andrew a text.

Congratulations, you just starred in my quickest jerk off session ever.

His reply came through when I was on my way to get breakfast.

I read your text and almost crashed the car.

I dialled his number. "Are you okay?"

He laughed. "Yes, I'm fine. But I still hate you."

I grinned into the phone. "No you don't."

His voice was much softer when he replied. "No, I really don't."

TWELVE

"LOOK AT YOU, ALL GRINNING AWAY TO YOURSELF," Lola said with a smile. "I take it you and Andrew...?" She trailed off suggestively and waggled her eyebrows.

I looked up from the delivery orders I was marking off against the invoices. "Andrew and I had our first fight."

She stopped, and her smile turned to a look of confusion. "What?"

"Well, I guess it was a fight. It was kind of... I'm not sure, to be honest."

"But you made up?"

"Oh, yeah," I answered, slowly nodding my head. "Relationships are weird."

"What was it about?"

I launched into full disclosure of how the whole night went, from seeing Lance at the bookstore up to me getting out of the cab and refusing to let Andrew walk away.

Gabe nodded sympathetically. "I couldn't tell you how many times I've had to go mow down Lola because she's pissed at me and won't talk about it."

"Too pissed off to talk," she amended, not so gently.

"It's what relationships are," Gabe said. "Weird, hard, and a lot of work."

"You make it sound like a job," she replied. "Is it not worth it?"

Gabe smiled at her and said, "Lola, my sweetest love, I would endure the wrath of eternal hell in exchange for just one day with you."

She grinned at him, then looked at me. "See? That is what we like to call a correct answer."

She gave Gabe a kiss on the cheek and shoved a make-up kit into my hands. "You ready?"

"Yep." Then I amended, "I am ready for you to drive me to find this Yanni guy. I am not ready to die in a car called Cindy Crawford."

Lola glared at me. "I hear the buses are running on time."

I laughed and headed for the door. "Andrew said something similar this morning."

POL'S ACADEMY OF ACTING AND FILM WAS SMALL, AND if the first college looked like a university, this looked more like a government department office or even a health clinic. It was older, clearly had less-to-no funding, or could have possibly been a volunteer-run class. Even wearing Andrew's old trousers and a simple T-shirt, I was overdressed. If Yanni had left the first college for this one, whatever the reason, it couldn't have been good.

The size and administration held one thing in my favour: trying to find someone shouldn't be hard.

After a quick look around, I found a class roster on the corkboard in the main admin area. No names of students of course, but teachers and the names of classes and the times they were run. I hung around and waited as students came in and out, and class after class finished, but I didn't see anyone that resembled him. When I'd been there for a few hours, one of the students—a young guy of about eighteen with long hair and holes in his sneakers—took pity on me. "You look lost," he said.

I gave him my best friendly smile. "I'm actually waiting for someone. I'm not even sure if I'm in the right place."

He looked around. "Well, this is Pol's, and all there is to it. It's not like you can get lost here."

I laughed and acted a bit nervous. "Do you know a Yanni Tomaras?"

The guy looked at me for a second. "Yeah, I think so."

I sat back and sighed, giving my best impression of someone who was happy to sit and wait. "Well, at least I'm in the right place."

Then the guy called out to someone else. "Hey Gary? Seen Yanni today?"

The guy called Gary replied, "Nah, not yet. He's in at four for improvs, I think."

I checked my watch. It was half past two. "Okay, sweet," I said. "Thanks."

"Sure thing," the first guy said as he walked out with his group of friends, seemingly not giving me another thought as they walked out discussing the class they'd just finished.

So I waited.

And sure enough, at five to four a guy matching Yanni's description came in. It was him. It had to be. Tall, olive skin, and green eyes, good looking, despite the sadness in his features. I was just about to stand and approach him when some girl called his name. *Yanni.* He turned, and they made small talk as they walked into a classroom.

So I'd found him. It hadn't strictly been difficult, and I wondered what the deal was with Lance.

Was he really that clueless? Or did he just want someone to do his dirty work for him? Or did it have to be completely off the grid because he'd had restraining orders put out against him? I really had no clue.

For any other job, I'd have called my client straight away and told them I'd made contact or even just a general update, but calling Lance was the last thing I intended to do. Not until I spoke to Yanni first.

And right on five o'clock, students filed out of the class-rooms, Yanni being at the tail end. Most of the other students had gone by the time he came out alone.

"Yanni?" I called his name.

He stopped, jerkily, suddenly halting. He almost took a step backward. "Who wants to know?"

"Someone asked me to find you," I said. "Just to see if you were okay. They were worried."

He shook his head, but I could see him eye the exit doors to the street. "Who?"

"Lance Nader."

Yanni turned white; the colour literally drained from his face. And I knew, without one iota of doubt, it was Lance all along. "It's not your father," I mumbled. "It's him."

His voice cracked in a barely audible whisper. "How did you find me?"

"He asked me to track you down," I said. Yanni looked like he was about to vomit. I put my hands up. "No, no. I didn't know. He lied to me. Everything he said was a lie."

"He knows where I am?"

"No."

He shook his head. He was tearing up, suddenly sweating and now a shade of green. He spoke more to himself than to me. "I can't afford to transfer out again. I quit my job. I had to. I moved, I've got no money. If he's found me..."

I shook my head and put my hand out to touch his arm but stopped myself. He flinched anyway. "I don't think so. Jesus, I'm sorry. I had no idea. He told me he was concerned for your welfare. He told me he thought your father was abusive. But it was him, wasn't it? That arsehole."

Yanni laughed, it sounded one beat away from crazy. "My father?" He shook his head, but then it seemed that words failed him. He started to breathe erratically, and a fine sweat now covered his still-pale face. If I had wondered why he didn't run, it was because I doubted his ability to even breathe properly at this point.

I couldn't just leave him. He was having a panic attack because that arsehole ex-boyfriend was the abuser. I knew something was off with that guy. I should have trusted my instincts and told him to fuck off two minutes into our first meeting. Instead, I'd found the poor guy and ruined his feeble attempt at a new life. "Yanni, you have to understand. I didn't know. He lied to me."

"Did he... has he hurt you?" he asked in a wheezy whisper.

"No, it's not like that with me. Yanni, is there someone I can call for you?"

He put his hand to his heart and shook his head again. "No... be okay," he said, struggling to breathe.

"I'm not leaving you until I know you're safe," I said to him. "How about we sit down and you catch your breath. I'll wait with you."

He didn't exactly agree with me, but he certainly didn't object. I pointed toward a bench seat in the waiting room, and he nodded before walking over and all but falling onto it. He put his head in his hands, and I sat beside him, waiting while he got himself together the best he could.

"He doesn't know where I am?" he asked again. "Why did you find me?"

"No. He doesn't know where you are. I haven't told him anything because he's shady as hell. He asked me to look for you. He said he was in love with you and he was worried, but I never told him anything because I had a feeling something was off with him."

All Yanni could do was blink, and I doubted he'd heard a word after 'No.' I'd had freak-outs before and I knew they were different for everyone, but for me I just needed someone close by. Not touching me, not telling me to calm down or take deeper breaths or smothering me or getting in my personal space. I just needed to *not* be alone. So that's what I did with him.

I waited until he was ready to talk. If talking was even what he wanted to do. I just sat next to him and watched the college kids coming and going, just hoping that no one stopped to ask if he was all right. Thankfully, no one did.

I was good at waiting for people to speak first. I just wasn't really expecting him to say what he did. "Did he follow you here?"

"What?" I said, before I could stop myself. "No. Well, I don't think so." Jesus. What kind of guy were we really dealing with?

Yanni swallowed hard and looked at me then. I could see the fear in his eyes. "I can't stay here."

"Okay," I said. "Where can I take you? Tell me, and I'll get you there."

He looked around the communal waiting room, like he was surprised to find himself there. "Um, I'm staying at a hostel. I didn't really have anywhere else to go." He looked as though he was going to be sick again.

"Yanni. My name is Spencer Cohen. Will you let me take you somewhere safe?"

He stared at me, his eyes wide, and he turned from white back to green. "Will you take me to him?"

"No, no," I put my hands up. "Jesus, no. Yanni, I had no idea. He lied to me. He asked me to find you. He told me he was concerned for your welfare. He told me your family harmed you when they found out you were seeing another man."

Yanni gave a laugh that sounded a little manic. "Well, that much was true. But it was nothing compared to what…" His words ran out of steam as the first of his tears fell. "I don't have anyone."

This guy was me. He had lived through what I lived through. Only I found my own family in Lola and Emilio. Yanni found a closed fist and god knows what else in the arms of that monster, Lance.

"Yanni, I know what it's like to be alone. I really do. My parents disowned me, kicked me out, and cut me out of their lives completely when I was sixteen. I can't help you with your family. But I can help you with Lance. I can make sure you're not alone. I didn't realise what my finding you would mean, so please let me make this right. For tonight at least. We can work something out tomorrow, but tonight you won't have to sleep in fear, okay?"

Fresh tears fell, as though my words struck a chord. He scrubbed his face with his hands, he clenched his jaw, and his nostrils flared as though he was trying to summon every ounce of strength he could muster from that place down deep that people seldom knew of. And he nodded. It was the tiniest of head movements, and with that simple gesture, without a word, without another move, he was putting his hand up for help.

And that was a strength I'd never known.

"Okay, thank you, Yanni. I'll just call my friend Lola. She'll come get us and take us back to my place. We can work out where to go from there, but at least you won't be here, okay?"

He barely nodded.

I pulled out my phone and hit Lola's number. "You'll love Lola. She's tiny, has pink hair, pretty as a 50s pin-up girl, but she's a fierce and protective friend. She also drives like a crazy person, dances like a ballerina, but sings like a scalded cat. Don't tell her I said that."

I got a small smile from Yanni just as Lola answered the phone. "Spencer?"

"Hey, how far away are you?"

"Five minutes. Everything okay?"

"Kind of. I'll explain when we get in the car."

"We?"

"I found Yanni, and I'm taking him to my place." Yanni's gaze shot to mine, so I took his hand and gave it a reassuring squeeze. I looked at Yanni. "Is there a back access door or something here?"

He nodded, and a little colour had returned to his face. "I think it's Union Parade," he said.

"Lola, can you come round the back? Yanni thinks it's called Union Parade, but I'm not sure."

"I'll find it. See you soon," was all she said.

There was about five seconds silence after I pocketed my phone. "Yanni, please know I'm very sorry. I didn't mean to scare you."

That's when his tears started.

And they didn't seem to stop.

I took his hand and led him through what I hoped was the rear of the building out the fire escape doors to the street that ran along the back of the building. And just a minute later, Cindy Crawford came careening down the street. Lola stopped the car, took one look at the crying kid with me, and never said a word.

I sat in the back with him, not sure what else I should do. I didn't want to crowd him, but I didn't want him to be alone either. Lola kept her eyes on me in the rear vision mirror instead of the road, and how on earth she could drive I'll never know. But when we pulled out onto the Boulevard, she started to talk.

She told us about her afternoon, the job, the models, the photographers, the passers-by, every minute little detail that she normally wouldn't speak of. She just kept talking, for whose comfort I wasn't sure.

I'm fairly certain Yanni never heard a word of it. He just stared into space, yet his tears never stopped. And I think that's what scared Lola the most.

Silent tears are the worst. It's the sign of a broken spirit. No sound, no residual emotions... just tears. Silent, unstoppable tears.

This poor kid—really only a few years younger than me, but he seemed like a kid to me. Helpless, defenceless, in need of protection—so completely vulnerable, that getting into a car with two complete strangers was a better alternative to where he thought Lance might find him. He couldn't have known coming with us would be any better, but the need to keep moving was an ingrained self-defence manoeuvre. Maybe he didn't care anymore. Maybe he was resigned to being handed back to the monster who abused him. I couldn't think of anything else to do, but I reached over and held his hand.

I don't think he noticed.

LOLA PARKED OUT THE BACK OF EMILIO'S SHOP, AND I led a dazed and confused Yanni up to my flat. It was just on five thirty so there was plenty of light. Too much light actually, so I pulled down the blind over the window that fronted Abbot Kinney Boulevard and offered Yanni the papasan chair. I got him a bottled water and pulled the blanket off the lounge and put it over Yanni's lap, and within seconds, he was curled up, still staring into space.

I stood there not knowing what to say or do, feeling every bit helpless as I did years ago, and not even a minute later there was a knock at the door. Yanni startled, so I called out, "Who is it?"

"It's Emilio, man," the familiar voice called out.

I opened the door and Emilio came in, followed by Lola. "He insisted," she whispered.

Emilio looked at me, then back to the crumpled man on the round chair in front of the window. "Everything okay?" he asked quietly.

"I was right about Lance," I told him, loud enough for Yanni to hear. "It was him all along."

Emilio's jaw bulged and his nostrils flared. His dislike of a man he'd never even met was evident. Then Emilio walked over and knelt down in front of Yanni. He spoke softly, like he was talking to a frightened child. "You're safe here. Spencer's a good guy. We'll look after you, okay?"

Yanni barely nodded. He just pulled the blanket up and closed his eyes. I doubted it was to sleep, more to block the world around him out.

Emilio walked back over to me and whispered so Yanni couldn't hear. "He can't stay here."

Then, with the worst possible timing, there was another knock at the door. "Who is it?" I called out.

"Um, it's Andrew." There was a muffled sound, like he was mumbling something. "I can come back…"

I opened the door. He was a sight for sore eyes. God, I just wanted to throw my arms around him. I pulled him inside and did exactly that, but he was tense, and he didn't hug me back. When I pulled away, I saw he was staring at Emilio and Lola, and of course, the strange guy curled up on the papasan chair.

"That's Yanni," I said gently. "I was right about Lance."

A dozen emotions flickered across his face. "You found him," he murmured.

"As soon as I said that bastard's name, he freaked out. I had to bring him here." It was then I noticed Andrew was holding a vinyl album. "What's that?"

He stared at Yanni for a moment, then at the album jacket cover he was holding. "Oh, it's silly really. I wanted to get you something to say sorry for last night. It's some B-grade piano concerto of Jeff Buckley's 'Hallelujah.'" He shrugged. "I had to make some calls to find it… I just think flowers aren't very personal, and I wanted to say sorry."

Despite the crazy, emotional afternoon, all I could do was laugh quietly, because that right there, was proof this beautiful man understood me. I put my hands to his face and drew him in for a kiss.

Andrew blushed at my display of affection in front of Emilio and Lola, but he couldn't take his eyes off Yanni. He whispered, "Is he okay?"

"He will be."

"It was the boyfriend?"

I nodded. "I've never seen someone so scared," I whispered. "And I only mentioned his name."

Andrew nodded sadly.

I sighed heavily. "I didn't know where else to take him. I couldn't just leave him there."

"I don't think he should stay here," Emilio said. "If Lance found out, he could come looking for him, especially if he knows where you live."

"I never told him where I live," I replied.

Lola frowned and asked, "What about Gerard, your old client? Didn't he recommend Lance to you? Did he come here when you worked with him?"

I shook my head. "Never. I met him at cafés or bars. I never brought any of my clients here. Well, except for Andrew."

Lola gave me a small smile, though she still looked concerned. "I agree with Emilio. If Yanni thought Lance might have followed you—" She shook her head. "Spencer, the guy's a bastard. There's no saying what he will or won't do."

Andrew looked at each of us, then back at Yanni. "I know where he can stay."

I shook my head. "He's not staying with you. I don't want you implicated in this in any way."

Andrew shook his head and gave me a small smile. "No. Somewhere else."

THIRTEEN

WE BUNDLED YANNI INTO ANDREW'S CAR, AND AFTER saying goodbye to Emilio and Lola, Andrew drove us out into the neon lit LA night. Wherever he was taking us was familiar to him, and the further he drove, the lights dulled from city neon to residential. But not just any residential. Oh no, these were the houses of the rich and famous. I recognised some of the street names from movies, and before long, Andrew pulled up to a large gate and entered in a security code. The gate slid open, and he drove forward, pulling up at the front door.

Okay then. This was a part of Andrew I had no clue about.

He climbed out of the driver's seat and opened Yanni's door. "It's a secure house. No one gets in or out without a security code."

Yanni, who had barely spoken a word since this afternoon, got out of the car. He was wooden, which I imagined was exhaustion. He could barely keep his eyes open, and I wondered how long it had been since he'd had a restful sleep.

The front door to the house opened. "Andrew?"

I turned to see his mother standing in the doorway, looking as glamorous as before. This was his parents' house? *Jesus Christ!*

She looked at her son and at me, then at Yanni before going back to Andrew. "Everything okay, Andrew?" she asked.

"No," he replied simply. "Can we come in?"

She stood aside. "Of course, please do."

Andrew led the way, and we found ourselves in a large, expensively furnished lounge room, or was it a sitting room? I had no idea what to call these rooms in American houses. My parents and Aunt Marvie had a front formal sitting room, if that's what this was. It was then I saw Yanni was staring at Andrew's mother. He took an unsteady breath and looked to the floor. "Mrs Helen Landon, it's an incredible honour."

Okay, so I was lost. "You know his mother?" The words were out before my stupid brain could stop them.

Yanni nervously shot me a quick glance. "I'm sorry. I assumed everyone did. I apologise if I was out of place," he whispered so damn brokenly it was like a slap to the face. What the hell had this guy been through?

"It's okay, my dear," Mrs Landon replied. "I still get recognised."

Recognised. I looked around the room, then paying better attention, found a slew of statues and awards on the mantel. Then I recalled Andrew saying something about his parents being 'theatre people.' And Yanni was an acting student... "Oh."

Andrew fought a smile beside me, but he was quickly serious again. "Mom, Yanni here is in some danger. He left an abusive relationship, but the guy is trying to find him. He needed somewhere safe to stay. I hope you don't mind?"

His mother blinked at Andrew, then turned to Yanni. He had gone pale again, like the admission out loud brought with it a fresh wave of memories. She slowly put her hand on his arm and urged him to sit on the sofa, cautiously sitting down beside him. "I don't mind at all. Andrew, be a dear and make a fresh pot of coffee. Decaf, please."

Andrew turned and walked out through a different door, and I saw it was my cue to give Andrew's mum and Yanni some time alone. It also gave me some time to get my head around everything. The kitchen was huge and grand, much like the rest of the house, I'd imagine. Andrew used the kitchen like it was his own, familiar with where everything was. "I grew up in this house," he said, reading my curious face.

"Your mum is someone famous?" I asked. "I didn't recognise her, sorry. She must think I'm an arse."

He chuckled quietly. "She's in theatre. She's done some Broadway." He fixed the coffee, and with a heavy sigh, he said, "Her first husband was a horrible man. He was violent and—" He shook his head. "Anyway, she managed to leave him. But she's never hid what she went through. Not to us, anyway. She would tell us so that if we ever found ourselves in a similar situation, that we'd never be too scared to ask for help."

"Fuck."

He nodded again, and this time managed a small smile. "She will help him."

I really wasn't quite sure what to say. "Andrew, I had no idea."

Just then, we saw headlights of a car through the kitchen window. Andrew craned his neck to see who it was. "It's my dad."

Oh. In what had been a head-spinning day, I wasn't sure I was up for meeting Andrew's father.

"Hey," Andrew whispered. He took hold of my hand and waited until I looked in his eyes. "I know it's probably too soon to be meeting my dad, but I think today's been a little out of the ordinary, right? And you've already met my mom twice, and that went okay."

"But he's your father."

"So?"

"It's different," I admitted. I don't know why meeting his father was any different to meeting his mother. It just was.

Andrew knew, apparently. He put his hand to my cheek and spoke with a reverence, a surety I didn't even know I needed. "He's my father, not yours. He will accept you because you're in my life. That's the only reason he needs."

I didn't have time to respond, even if I could have made my stupid brain come up with something remotely worthy. A door closed not too far away, and someone was whistling a happy tune. "Andrew?" a man called out, and he stopped when he walked into the kitchen through a different door we'd come through. Clearly Andrew's father, he was almost identical to him, albeit some twenty-odd years older. Blond, handsome, with kind blue eyes. "Saw your car out front," he said, putting his wallet and keys in the fruit bowl on the kitchen counter.

"Hey, Dad," Andrew said. "Dad, this is Spencer. Spencer, this is my dad, Allan."

Allan Landon extended his hand and a warm smile. "Ah, the one I've heard all about," he said, shaking my hand firmly.

"Spencer Cohen," I offered, thankful I seemed to hide my nerves in front of him.

He turned back to Andrew, then clearly knowing his son very well, he frowned. "What's up?"

"We brought someone here with us," Andrew said. "He's in the lounge room with Mom. He's in a bit of trouble, Dad. He needed somewhere safe to stay, so I brought him here."

Allan's expression softened. "Explains the coffee, huh? Better make me a cup. Bring it in for us, won't you?"

Andrew smiled at him. "Sure thing."

I watched Andrew's father leave via the door we'd come through, stunned at his total acceptance and ability to not bat an eyelid at the news there was a troubled stranger in the front room. Let alone his son's new boyfriend in his kitchen. "Just like that, huh?" I whispered.

Andrew put his hand on my chest and stared at me for a long second. "Just like that."

A sudden ache in my heart, like an axe through my chest, made me think of my own father. Of how simple total acceptance was assumed in Andrew's life, and how I had struggled and fought for—and was denied—the same thing. His parents rolled with it, took it in stride, and even went out of their way to help a young gay man in need, where my family had done the exact opposite. Except my parents hadn't turned away a gay stranger. They'd turned away their own son.

Andrew's hand crept up to my neck, and he pulled me into a kiss. "Just like that," he said again. "Just like it should be."

When the coffee was done, Andrew balked at pouring the fifth cup. "Shit," he mumbled. "There's no tea. I'm sorry. I forgot."

"Coffee's fine," I told him. "I'm sure I'll survive."

He fixed the cups on a tray with sugar and cream and carried it in to the front sitting room. Mrs Landon still sat beside Yanni, and Mr Landon sat across from him, elbows on his knees, listening intently to what Yanni was telling them. I sat on the single seat sofa, and Andrew sat on the arm rest at my side, and we listened to Yanni talk.

"It's so cliché," Yanni said softly. "But he really was charming in the beginning. I didn't even realise he'd isolated me. In the six months I was living with him, I had no friends, no one but him." Yanni shook his head. "I really was so naïve."

Mrs Landon put her hand on his arm. "No you weren't," she said. Her voice was soft but determined. "The fault is his, not yours."

Yanni's eyes welled with tears. "Then he started to get possessive and mad if I was late." He swallowed hard. "The first time he hit me, he'd been stressed at work, and he was so sorry, and I believed him." He scrubbed at his tears. "I'm sorry."

"Don't apologise," Mr Landon said gently. "You're allowed to cry. You've lost a lot. You need to grieve for that."

Yanni stared at him. Like stared. And he was right, Yanni had lost a lot. Not material things, but emotionally and psychologically, Yanni had lost it all. And something about that realisation, and how Mr Landon spoke something so profound, like it was the easiest thing in the world to say, made my chest hurt.

Somehow, like he knew what I was thinking and feeling, Andrew took my hand and gave it a squeeze. He didn't let it go.

"He paid for me to go to college, something I could never do on my own. I lived in his expensive apartment. And at first it was exciting, that I could do these things because I had no money, no family," Yanni said. He looked right at me and I nodded. I had told him I'd lost my family, and I'd thought he hadn't heard me. He obviously had. It was a look that Andrew's parents didn't miss, and they both saw how Andrew was holding my hand.

"It took him less than twelve months to completely own me," Yanni said. He swallowed hard. His voice shook but he spoke anyway. "The last time he hit me, I swore it was the last time. I left with nothing. I had nothing. Everything I thought I had, was his. It was always his. I quit my job, I left school. I left my cell phone that he'd given me on the kitchen table and never went back. I stayed at a homeless shelter with my backpack and one change of clothes." He nodded at the bag at his feet. "I never thought I was a materialistic person until I had nothing."

I cleared my throat. "But those few things mean a lot. They're your worldly possessions, and they're everything."

Yanni nodded, and I knew all eyes were on me. Andrew squeezed my hand again. His thumb skimmed across my knuckles, such a reassuring gesture that kept me tethered to him. Without a word, he kept me afloat beside him instead of drowning in memories.

"Then you found me," Yanni said, still looking at me.

"I had no idea," I told him again. "Well, I knew something was off with him, but I didn't realise, and I'm so sorry to drag you back through this." I looked at Andrew's parents and explained, "Yanni's ex-boyfriend contacted me to find him. It's not what I usually do, but he lied so convincingly." I shook my head.

Yanni almost laughed. "He's a piece of work."

"But you went back to college?" Mrs Landon asked Yanni.

He nodded sadly. "He took everything, but I couldn't let him take that from me. Acting is what I do. It's the only good thing in my life. I left the Actors Academy and started at Pol's." He looked down at his hands. "It's not as revered or exclusive, but I'm doing it on my own, and that's more than he gave me."

Mrs Landon raised her chin and her eyes were glassy. She rubbed his arm. "Yanni, that is the sign of a true actor. One who fails to give up on his craft when he has nothing. That is a sure sign of strength and drive, and believe me, to make it in this industry you need both in spades."

"I can't go back to Pol's," he said. He shrugged again. "If he knows I went there."

"I never told him," I said adamantly. "I told him nothing. Actually, when I had a feeling he wasn't what he seemed, I told him you had a job in a bookstore in the city. We went to see if he turned up there looking for you."

"Did he?"

Andrew and I both nodded. "Yeah."

Yanni nodded knowingly, and his eyes welled with fresh tears. "He won't ever stop."

"Did you tell the police?" Andrew asked.

"Yes. I filed a restraining order, but it doesn't mean anything."

So, that made sense. "That's why he asked me and not the police or a detective agency."

Yanni put his untouched coffee back on the tray and sagged back into the sofa, and for a while no one spoke. Mr Landon broke the silence. "Yanni, when did you eat last?"

He shook his head and tried to recall, which was answer enough. Andrew's father stood. "I'll go see what I can find," he said as he walked toward the kitchen.

After a moment, Yanni shook his head and laughed in disbelief. He looked at Mrs Landon, and his hands started to shake as he wiped his face. "This is so surreal. I can't believe

I'm here sitting beside you, and *the* Allan Landon just offered to get me food. I don't know what I did to deserve this, or is there a Punk'd camera hidden somewhere?"

Andrew snorted. "No cameras. They're just my parents. Spencer said you needed help, so I helped."

Mrs Landon smiled at Andrew lovingly. She put her hand on Yanni's arm. "Yanni, I want to tell you something. I have been where you are. It was a long time ago before I met Allan. Actually, it was Allan who helped me leave my first husband."

Yanni stared at her.

She smiled at him. "I've known the fear and hopelessness you feel. That exhaustion you feel in your bones, I've felt that. You will get through it, if you let us help you."

He started to cry again, those silent, heartbreaking tears.

Mrs Landon kept on talking, "I'm on the board of directors at Acacia Foundation. It's a centre for men and women who are going through the same thing. We help people understand their legal rights and help them with police proceedings. We help them get back on their feet, find them somewhere to live, and employment placement."

Mr Landon came back into the room carrying another tray. Something on it smelled good. "It's just leftovers," he declared, putting the tray in front of Yanni. I doubted Yanni had seen that much food in days. It looked like a fajita mix of beef, rice, and vegetables with flat breads, and Yanni practically inhaled it. When he was done, he sagged back into his seat and closed his eyes.

"Come," Mr Landon said, standing up, waiting for Yanni to do the same. "You can sleep in the guest room, and we'll deal with tomorrow after breakfast."

Yanni picked up his backpack and followed Mr Landon obediently out of the room, and me, Andrew, and his mother watched in silence as they left.

I waited for Mrs Landon to look at me, and I said, "Thank you."

"You did the right thing," she said to the both of us. "We'll work out what he wants to do tomorrow." She looked at Andrew for a long moment, whether it was because he was still holding my hand, I wasn't sure. But it seemed to me she wanted a minute alone with him.

"I'll just take these trays back to the kitchen," I said, stacking cups and plates, then finally leaving them.

I placed all the dishes in the sink, then set about rinsing everything. Then I thought *fuck it* and filled the sink with hot water and detergent from under the sink and washed everything, and when that was done, I set about it drying it too. By then I'd run out of excuses for heading back in there, but I stopped at the door when I heard they were talking about me.

Mrs Landon said, "...you never mentioned his tattoos." My heart dropped.

"They're not just tattoos," Andrew told her. "They're scars. Scars made from ink. He wears them for the world to see as daily reminders of who he is. And anyway, I like them. His skin doesn't define him any more than mine defines me."

His mother was quiet for a moment, and I contemplated walking in there. Then she said, "He's a good man. If he was worried enough about a complete stranger to take him in, then that tells me all I need to know."

"He is, Mom. And he just gets me. He knew more about me in two days than Eli ever did."

"What's wrong then? Why are you so troubled over him?"

I almost put my fingertips through the drywall, waiting for him to answer.

"I'm trying to not rush this one, Mom. You know how I was with Eli."

"Spencer's different," she said. It wasn't a question.

"He is.

"You're in love with him."

Andrew didn't answer. There was only silence. Loud, deafening, heart-thumping silence. My stupid heart almost stopped in my chest. My stupid feet were bolted to the floor.

"It's written all over your face, Andrew," his mother said.

After the longest second, he answered. "I do."

And I finally breathed, relief and excitement and even a little nervous dread filled my entire body. My blood warmed and coursed erratically through my veins, and those foolish butterflies swarmed my throat. But the sound of a door closing nearby set my feet in motion, and I went back into the lounge room the same time Mr Landon did. "I think he's asleep already," he said.

I felt pale and clammy after hearing Andrew's admission—insecurities in my own worth manifested in physical traits—but if Andrew noticed, he didn't say. He stood and smiled at me. I wasn't sure what I should say or do now that we were alone with his parents, but I didn't have time to wonder for long. Andrew put his arm around my waist. "We'll get going, yes?"

"Yes, I'll make some phone calls," Mrs Landon said. "Pre-empt his needs, if he should decide to let us help him. The Foundation will find a spot for him."

"And if he doesn't want help?" I asked, without really meaning to.

"We can't help him if he doesn't want it," she said. "But he's safe tonight, and that's more than he had yesterday."

"I really am thankful," I told them. "I didn't mean for any of this to happen."

Andrew rubbed his hand on my back. "You did the right thing, Spencer."

His mother smiled kindly. "Can I get you boys something to eat?"

"No, Mom," Andrew said. "We'll get going. But I'll call you tomorrow to see how he's getting on."

She put her hand to Andrew's face. "Thank you for bringing him here. We'll look after him." Then she looked at me. "He said you wouldn't leave him."

I shook my head. "I couldn't. He's got no one, and I know what that's like."

She glanced at Andrew but smiled back at me. "You're a good one. I think it speaks volumes about character when one behaves in such a manner. But when you do such a kindness when no one is looking and there is no reward, it says even more." She kissed Andrew's cheek and whispered, "He's a keeper."

I almost died of blushing and swallowing my tongue, which only made her smile even more fondly at me. Mr Landon shook my hand again, then hugged Andrew before walking back into the kitchen.

Andrew's mother walked us to the door with her usual grace and elegance and waited until we were in the car. She waved as we drove down the drive, and only when we were through the security gates, did he hold out his free hand for me to hold. "You okay?"

"Yeah. You?"

"Yeah."

"What a day."

He smiled sadly at me. "A weird one, huh?"

"Just a little. Um, your parents..."

"My parents, what?"

"They're famous, or something."

He gave me a quiet laugh. "Or something. I told you they were in theatre."

"You didn't say they were famous."

"Well, they're not *that* famous. You didn't recognise them."

I groaned and put my free hand to cover my eyes. "They must think I'm some uncultured heathen. Were those like Oscars or Emmys on their mantel? I think I'll die if they are."

He laughed again. "Tonys. Well, one Tony among others."

I whined. I knew next to nothing about theatre acting, but even I knew what a Tony was. "Oh God."

Andrew squeezed my hand. "Poor Yanni thought he was on some episode of Punk'd."

"He recognised them straight away."

"He's studying stage acting, so I'm not surprised."

"Ugh. I'll have to apologise."

He laughed again. "No you won't. They liked you Spencer. In fact, I think they liked that you didn't have a clue who they were. Proof that you didn't want to be with me because of family connections. This is LA after all, where every second person is a next-big-thing wannabe."

I snorted. "Believe me, I can't act or sing."

He smiled at me as he drove. "They liked you just the way you are."

"They're remarkable people."

"They are. They do a fair bit of charity work and fundraising. The Acacia Foundation is my mother's brainchild."

I sighed and leaned back in my seat. My head was still swimming. This day had been a dozen emotions on repeat. Andrew went to a drive-thru and got us burgers and fries, and seeing Emilio's shop was shut and the lights were turned off, we went straight up to my flat. We fell on the couch and devoured our burgers. I moaned after the first bite. "Oh my God, this is soul food."

He laughed. "Saturated fats have healing properties," he said, shoving some fries in his mouth.

When I was done, as I cleaned up my flat, my safe haven, and had a belly full of food, my thoughts went back to Yanni. Andrew brought his empty drink into the kitchen. "Why the frown?" he asked softly.

"Just thinking."

"About Yanni?"

I nodded.

Andrew put his arms around me and held me tight. How he knew what I needed the moment I needed it, I'll never know, but I buried my face in his neck. "I've never seen someone so scared," I mumbled. "He was petrified."

Andrew pulled back and traced his thumb down the side of my face. "You saw yourself in him, didn't you?"

I stared at him. I felt stripped raw, skinless, and without any defences. But I nodded. "Yes."

He kissed me then, hard and soft at the same time, with a fierce but gentle fervour. He tasted of salt from the fries he'd eaten, but there was emotion on his tongue, in his hands, in the way he kissed me. And when he pulled back for a breath, his eyes were dark, and there was no mistake—no mistake at all—what he wanted.

I wanted it too. I wanted him to take me to bed, to be inside me. I wanted to feel the power and emotion of his entire body. I wanted to feel connected to him in every possible way.

Then I remembered…

Oh, fuck. I laughed and put my forehead to his cheek. "Oh, you're not going to believe this."

He looked at me, confused. "What?"

"I was going to buy condoms today on my way home. But then the whole Yanni thing happened and I forgot." I sighed, like the universe had conspired against me. "I don't have any here."

Andrew surprised me by laughing. "You know what?"

"The world hates me?"

He kissed me with smiling lips. "Well, there's that. But let's just go to bed anyway. Not for sex, let's just go to bed. Today's been... well, today's been... tiring."

I sighed. "It sure has."

As I flipped the lights off, I saw the vinyl record he'd brought with him when he turned up earlier. I'd forgotten about it. I slowly picked it up and looked at him. It was literally a dozen of my favourite songs played on piano. The most perfect gift from the most perfect guy, who had only a short while ago admitted to his mother that he was in love with me. A confession I still had to process. "Andrew." I swallowed hard. "I..." Unable to think, unable to speak, I just shook my head.

He took my hand and leaned against me. "I know," he whispered. "Spencer, I know." And with that, he took me to bed.

We stripped to our underwear, and we lay in the barely lit darkness. He rested his head on my chest and pulled my arm around his shoulder, where he took my arm and inspected it. "What does this tattoo mean?" he asked.

On my left forearm were six roses, drawn exactly opposite the ravens on my right arm. I explained the roses were for every year Aunt Marvie took me in. Above the roses were the words 'The Impossible Dream' for her favourite song. I explained the five stars in the Southern Cross formation was for Australia, and the compass was to remind me of the direction I was going.

He replied with soft kisses to my bare chest every so often, and when I was too tired to speak, he hummed my favourite song, "Hallelujah." And although I couldn't be sure, I think he skimmed his fingers across my chest like I was a piano, until I fell asleep.

And without my consent, with my defences in ruins, while my brain was sleeping, my stupid heart went and fell headfirst into love.

FOURTEEN

I woke up when Andrew knelt on the bed and kissed me goodbye. "I have to go home, grab my gear, and get my arse to the gym before work."

"Your arse can stay here," I said, barely able to open my eyes enough to see it was too early for coherent conversation.

He laughed and tweaked my nipple before he climbed off the bed. "Don't tempt me. I'll call you later. We still on for dinner tonight?"

The cogs in my mind turned over sleepily. Dinner... dinner... Friday night dinner. I was buying everyone dinner tonight. "Oh, yeah. Dinner. For sure."

"I'll just come by after work."

"Cool." I rolled over and pulled his pillow under my arm and hugged it instead.

"Don't get up or anything," he said sarcastically.

I didn't open my eyes. "No intention."

"I can see that." He climbed back on the bed, fully dressed, pressed his dick to my arse, and whispered in my ear. "Your mission for today, should you choose to accept it, is to buy some freakin' condoms."

Well, now I was awake.

I tried to roll over and grab him to keep him in bed, but he jumped back quickly. My arms caught nothing but air, and I fell heavily back onto the bed, exhausted at the effort. "I hate you."

He laughed as he walked out. "No you don't."

I heard the front door close, followed by silence. I was left alone with nothing but his lingering scent and his absence and a smile on my face. And raging morning wood, thanks to his dick against my arse. And a distant thought I couldn't quite remember, an inkling, not a memory, more of a feeling, tugged at my periphery.

Then it hit me, like a snowball to the face, or an armful of puppies, I couldn't quite decide. My last thought before falling asleep last night was a realisation that I was falling in love with Andrew.

Well, not me exactly. My stupid, traitorous heart. The very wall I'd built around my emotional wellbeing, made up of a patchwork of broken promises and blistering hurt, amongst other miscellaneous things, had sprung a leak.

I didn't know what to make of it. I didn't know what to do. I should have seen this coming when I'd decided to give this whole *boyfriends* thing a try. I should have known where it was headed.

To make myself vulnerable was something I swore I would never do to myself again. It was a survival thing. After I'd suffered an incomprehensible betrayal by those I loved the most, I promised myself to never let it happen again.

To trust someone with your heart was the most frightening thing a person could do. It wasn't just frightening, it was debilitating. My heart started to beat faster, almost to a panicked state. "Don't know why *you're* worried," I said out loud to my heart. "It's your fault we're in this mess."

Then I realised I'd just talked to my own heart like it was sitting beside me, and I wondered if my stupid brain had finally flipped its shit. I dug the heels of my hands into my eyes, two seconds away from calling for the white padded truck, when my phone beeped. I reached over and grabbed it only to see it was a message from Andrew.

> The drugstore down the road is open. I just drove past it.

I smiled at the screen, and my freak out lessened a bit. I quickly replied.

> Don't text and drive.

> I'm stuck at a stop light. Have you got them yet?

> I'm still in bed. Getting a little desperate, are we?

> No. Not a little. A lot.

I laughed.

> Shame you left. I guess I'll have to wank by myself.

His reply took a while.

> I hate you.

> No you don't.

And what I'd heard him tell his mother last night played through my mind. He loved me; he didn't hate me at all.

> This weekend I'll show you how much I hate you. You better buy in bulk.

I burst out laughing, my inner meltdown was almost forgotten.

> Deal.

A lot earlier than I normally got up, I rolled out of bed and took a shower, got dressed, and headed straight to the chemist. God forbid if I got side-tracked again and forgot to buy the condoms. Andrew'd never forgive me. I picked up the biggest pack they had, then thought better of it and grabbed a second pack as well. I was gonna hold him to this deal. We'd done well to make it to this weekend. I had high expectations and little doubt it was going to be worth every second.

I got back home and threw the package on my bed. Two bulk packs of frangers and a bottle of lube and a pack of jelly beans spilled out on the still-rumpled sheets. I snapped a pic on my phone and sent it to him.

> My end of the deal is complete. Now you just need to hold up your end of the deal.

He didn't reply for an hour or so, and when my phone beeped, I was downstairs explaining to Emilio and Daniela what had happened when we took Yanni to Andrew's parents' house. I took out my phone, and I guessed, looking at the clock, that Andrew would have just gotten to work after the gym.

> What's the candy for?

> Stamina. Yours, not mine.

When I re-pocketed my phone, both Emilio and Daniela were staring at me. I tried to wipe the smile off my face. They both gave me fond smiles, kinda like I'd imagine proud parents would look at their kid when they were all grown up. "What?"

Emilio shook his head slowly. "You have it bad, my friend."

I groaned. "I'm trying not to think about that, thanks very much. I had a minor freak out this morning, and I might have heard Andrew tell his mother last night that he was in love with me, and my stupid brain packed up and left—"

"Wait, what?" Daniela interrupted. "You heard Andrew say what?"

I buried my face in my hands. "Ugh. I don't know. I'm trying to figure out what to say to this arsehole Lance." I looked at the clock again. How was it just nine o'clock? "I've been up for hours already. Normally I'm not even out of bed yet. I don't even know what the fuck I'm doing."

Daniela put both hands on my shoulders. "Breathe, Spencer."

I took a deep breath, and it was funny. I didn't remember not breathing, but I clearly needed to. I felt a bit better.

"Of course he loves you," she said, her eyes full of kindness. "And it's okay to let yourself love him too. He's a good man, a kind heart."

I tried to answer, to object, but my realisation that I might already love him stayed unsaid. It was one thing to admit it to myself, but to say it out loud made that shit real. As if the universe had some no take-backs, no returns clause, like kids in a playground.

Daniela put her hand to my cheek and said something in Spanish, which I didn't understand. Then she said it in English, "You deserve him."

I filled my lungs with the deepest breath I could manage and let it out slowly, trying to stave off the impending panic attack.

"Okay," Emilio said, clapping his hands together. He must have known I needed a change of direction in conversation. "Let's discuss our plans for Lance."

I looked at him, confused. "Our plans?"

He grinned. "Of course, brother. I think some Mexican persuasion might be in order."

Now I was really lost. "What?"

"Anyone who hits the person they're supposed to love—man, woman, makes no difference—needs a lesson in how to show some respect. We should teach him the Mexican way."

I was almost afraid to ask. "Do I even want to know what that means?" I'd never known Emilio to be aggressive in any way. "You're not seriously talking about roughing this guy up?"

He laughed. "Give me some credit, my friend. Call Lance the Tosser. Make an appointment to see him, and we'll go pay him a visit at his work, yeah? I'll get my cousins to come with us. It'll be fun."

I stared at him.

Emilio held out his fist. "Trust."

I had no clue what I was in for, but I trusted Emilio implicitly. I bumped my fist to his. "Trust."

AFTER I'D HELPED LOLA MOST OF THE MORNING, I left a message for Andrew to call me in his lunch break, and three hours later my phone rang. "Hey, what's up?"

Just hearing his voice made me smile. "Have you heard

from your parents? I was just wondering how Yanni was doing."

"I have. I spoke to my mom earlier. She said he was much better this morning. They think they've found him a place, but Mom doesn't want to rush him. I think she likes him. She was very impressed with his dedication to acting."

"Did she mention Lance and what Yanni wanted to do?"

"Well, Lance asking you to find him was a breach of his restraining order conditions, directly or indirectly. I can't remember what she said exactly. He wasn't too keen on going back to the police, but my mother can be pretty persuasive." Andrew took a breath. "Can I ask why?"

"I'm going to see him."

"Oh, Spencer, I don't think that's a good idea," he started to say. "The guy is clearly not stable."

"Emilio's coming with me," I told him. "It's going to be epic."

"Do I want to know?"

I laughed. "Probably not. I'll tell you all about it tonight."

"Please be safe."

I sighed into the phone. "I will be. And thank you. For worrying, I guess."

He answered with a smile in his voice. "No problem. *I guess.*"

After we'd said goodbye, I slid my phone into my pocket and looked at the three guys coming with me. Emilio and his two cousins Ricky and Paul. Emilio was the most placid, friendliest, family-oriented guy I knew. I doubted he could even hurt a fly. But seeing him and his cousins wearing the black suits they wore to their grandfather's funeral, with their hair slicked back and tattoos visible up their necks and on their knuckles, I had to admit, they looked pretty badass.

Emilio grinned at me. "You ready?"

"Hell yes I am."

"Wait!" Daniela cried. "I need to get photos. You guys look great!"

Some happy snaps later we left, and on the drive into the city, I told Ricky and Paul what I knew, considering they were now helping us. I'd made an appointment to see Lance in his office. His personal assistant didn't seem too happy about it, but when she told Lance my name, he said he'd see me. I might have omitted the fact I was bringing company.

Emilio had asked his cousins to join him. Both heavily tattooed, Ricky was a baker by trade and Paul worked as a courier driver, both nice guys who worked early mornings and had afternoons free. As soon as Emilio had asked for their help and told them briefly why, they didn't even hesitate.

I had to force myself not to smile as we walked into Lance's city building. I wore my usual chinos but added a jacket, though I doubted anyone noticed or cared about me. It was the three Mexican-mafia-looking dudes who flanked me most people balked at.

Lance's assistant stared at us as we approached her desk. "Spencer Cohen," I told her with my usual disarming smile. Emilio, Ricky, and Paul stood back with stoic faces, and the poor startled woman eyed the briefcase Emilio held. It held some papers and a few tattoo magazines in case x-ray machines thought an empty case was suspicious, but she didn't know that. "I'm here for a three o'clock meeting with Lance."

"Of course," she whispered. She pressed a button on her phone. "Spencer Cohen is here to see you."

"Send him in," he replied curtly.

She led us to his door, and slimy Lance smiled when he

saw me. It quickly slid off his face when Emilio, Ricky, and Paul walked in behind me.

It was a nice office with a pretty decent view of the city, and the glass interior walls gave his colleagues full view of us.

And they were watching.

Lance still stood behind his desk, I planted myself in the chair directly across from him, Emilio sat beside me, and Ricky and Paul stood at the door, their tattooed hands clasped in front, and they stared straight ahead. Emilio put the briefcase on the desk. I crossed one ankle across my knee—looking as relaxed as could be—while Lance struggled to sit in his chair. "Spencer...?" He cleared his throat. "What can I do for you?"

"Nice office," I said, nodding slowly and taking my time to look around. I made a point of looking at his watching colleagues, just in case he wasn't aware they were staring. "I found Yanni."

The piece of shit swallowed hard, and his eyes shifted nervously. "How is he?"

"Oh, he's fine. Now. He's in a safe house where you can't ever find him."

Lance blanched. He knew. He knew we knew the truth. He shook his head. "It's not like that."

"It's exactly like that," I said. "What did you think would happen? Did you think I'd willingly drag a lamb back to slaughter? Or did you do it just to fuck with his head? Or just because you could? Is it a power thing? Is that what you think? That it would have been quicker to lure Yanni back in rather than lure in some other unsuspecting kid you could belt the shit out of to make yourself feel better?"

Lance paled. "I'll call security," he said weakly.

I laughed and sat back in my chair. "That's right. You would. Because you're a coward. Only a coward, a spineless fucking coward, would ever raise his fist in anger to someone smaller, weaker..." I sneered at him. "Yet you'd squeal for help when you felt threatened. You're a worthless piece of shit."

He gaped like a fish, pale and clammy.

I sighed. "The police have been notified that you breached the restraining order Yanni placed against you. You can probably expect a visit."

He instinctively looked out the glass partition wall toward the elevators.

"And I will happily give them every email and text you sent me if I'm subpoenaed to do so. So, I'll tell you what's going to happen," I said, like I was bored with the whole thing. "You're going to forget Yanni. Don't even look for him, or we will know. In fact, if you ever abuse *anyone*, physically harm them or fuck with their mental wellbeing, we will know."

Lance looked at Ricky and Paul nervously.

He was sweating now and looked about ready to piss himself. I didn't care.

"It's been psychologically proven that people who perpetuate domestic violence have very little self-worth, debilitating insecurities, and are sometimes impotent or have very small dicks." I looked at Emilio and shrugged. "Or so I read."

Emilio nodded seriously. "I believe I read that also."

I pretended to pull at a thread on the hem in my pants. "So Lance, here's where you promise, like the piece of shit, small-dicked man you are, that you will leave Yanni alone. Forever."

Lance nodded.

"Say it," I prompted.

"Okay, okay," he said.

"Good," I said with a smile. "I'm glad you agree."

Emilio stared him down. "You know, in Mexico we have a saying. *Lo prometido es deuda*," he said, his accent thick and clipped. Then he repeated it in English. "What has been promised, is debt." He stared at Lance until the piece of shit squirmed in his seat. "Don't make us come collect. Because we will."

I stood up and Emilio did too, and Lance followed on what I could only assume was shaky legs. I held out my hand for him to shake, more on my side of his table because there was no way I was meeting this fucker half way on anything. He hesitantly leaned across and shook my hand. His palm was sweaty and limp, his face still pale. "Now, smile for your colleagues who are watching. And get yourself some help. See a shrink that deals with abusive arseholes like yourself. For fuck's sake."

We left, I gave the wide-eyed assistant a smile as we walked past, and it wasn't until we were in the elevator and the doors closed that we all busted up laughing. "Man, you were so good!" I told Emilio. I slapped my hand to his. "Don't make us come collect," I mimicked his voice.

Emilio grinned proudly. "And you telling him he's a piece of shit, small-dicked man." He laughed some more. "Perfect."

"I speaketh the truth," I said. "So, do you reckon it worked? You think he'll look for Yanni now?"

Emilio shook his head as we walked out onto the city sidewalk. "Nah. Like you said. That piece of shit is a fucking coward."

I held my fist out for him to bump with his. "Like I said, my man, I only speaketh the truth."

WE WERE STILL PUMPED LATER THAT NIGHT, SITTING around the small waiting room in the tattoo parlour. It was after seven, Emilio had shut the shop early, and the table in the middle of the chairs was filled with an array of takeout containers. Lola and Gabe were there, Daniela and Emilio, and me. I was waiting for Andrew to arrive, and right on seven, my phone beeped. He was at the back door. I let him in with a kiss. He dropped an overnight bag inside the door, and we walked through to where everyone was chatting, laughing, and eating. I pulled him onto the sofa next to me, sitting so our sides touched, shoulder to shoe.

When we'd got back from our little visit with Lance, I'd sent Andrew a text to say everything went as planned. But now we filled him in on the details. Daniela handed Andrew her phone with the photo we'd taken before we'd left, suited up with our game faces on. "That's them, all dressed up."

Andrew looked at the picture and his gaze shot to Emilio. "Is that you?"

It was hard to reconcile the mean looking guy in the photo to the always smiling, happy-faced Emilio sitting across from us. "Impressive, huh?"

"You look *good!*" Andrew said, then of course he blushed when everyone laughed. "I didn't mean it like that."

Emilio held his fist out for Andrew to bump. "Thanks, my man." Then he turned to Daniela. "See? I am good looking to everyone, not just the ladies."

And we spent the next several hours talking, laughing, eating, and drinking beers. Emilio and Andrew had drawing contests, most of which ended in bursts of laughter, and I spent the night with my hand on his thigh, chatting with everyone, marvelling at how perfect this was.

Andrew, the unlikeliest of people, a proper-speaking,

argyle-wearing nerd fit in with this bunch of tattooed, mismatched family like he was made just for it.

Like he was made just for me.

I hadn't realised it was so late, but when Andrew looked at his watch, he smiled. "It's Saturday."

I shook my head, a little confused. "So?"

He narrowed his eyes at me and whispered, "So? That means it's Saturday. And you never specified what time on Saturday we had to wait until. And I'm not waiting until Saturday night. No way."

Saturday? "Oh."

Andrew stood up. "Thank you all for a great night," he said, "but we might be going now."

I laughed from where I still sat on the sofa. "It's possible I told them we were holding off until this weekend before we had sex."

Andrew stared at me, his mouth fell open, and he blushed right down his neck; his cheeks and the tips of his ears went red. He closed his eyes for a second then sighed loudly. "Well, on that note, yes, it's now technically the weekend," he checked his watch again, "by one minute. So we have somewhere else we'd rather be, no offence."

I laughed, got to my feet, and put my arms around him. "Your tact could use some work."

Andrew shrugged and half-smiled. He ran his hand over my arse. "You're wasting time."

I laughed again and turned to our somewhat shocked friends. "He doesn't look like the bossy type, does he?"

Lola laughed and clapped her hands together. "You tell him, Andrew. And Spencer, we don't want to see you until Sunday morning coffee."

Andrew took my hand and dragged me toward the back

door. "Don't worry, you won't," he called out, and I could still hear them laughing as we shut the door behind us.

He had his overnight bag and waited for me to open the door. I let him inside first and followed him in, where he dropped his bag and pushed me against the door with his body. He kissed me like no one else had ever kissed me. He was ravenous, demanding, and so fucking hot. When he finally pulled his mouth from mine, he whispered against my mouth, "I've waited so long for this."

My dumbarse brain was still reeling from that kiss. "Me too."

"Tell me right now if you don't want this," he said, still pushing me up against the door. His hard on rubbed against mine, his eyes were dark, his voice was gravel and honey.

"I want you, Andrew," I murmured against his lips. "I want you inside me, I want to feel you for days."

I felt him shudder as my words trickled down his spine. He groaned. "Fuck."

Then he took my hand and led me to my room.

FIFTEEN

There was no doubt about who was in charge. Andrew just took over, and I had no qualms in letting him. He pulled my shirt over my head and tossed it to the floor, then held my jaw while he kissed me. He decided the angle, he decided the depth, the tempo. Everything.

He ran his hand down my chest to my waistband and popped the fly. He slid my pants over my hips and palmed my dick. He bit back a groan and murmured, "Lie down."

I did, and he pulled my pants off by the hems at my ankles. Then he pulled off his own shirt, but his pants stayed on. He left me lying on the bed and walked casually around to the bedside table and found the condoms and lube, casting his eyes over me as he threw the foil packet and lube beside me.

I couldn't help but notice the very prominent bulge in his pants. "You're very overdressed," I said, languidly stroking myself.

He smirked as he undid his trousers and kicked them off. He was pale in the darkened room, standing naked and perfect, his cock jutted proudly from his body.

My blood warmed and my balls tightened as I looked at his erection, knowing exactly where it was about to go... my body ached with want.

"Andrew, please."

He knelt on the bed and edged up between my thighs and sat back on his knees. "I think we've left it too long," he mumbled. "This is going to be over very quickly."

"I don't care. I just want you inside me," I told him. "We have all weekend to get it right, so don't worry about that."

"I wasn't kidding when I said you'd be busy all weekend. I don't plan on leaving this room much at all."

I fisted my cock and swiped my palm over the head. Andrew pulled my hand away. "I believe your orgasm is my responsibility," he said with a smile as he gripped me.

I hissed, trying to stave off the pleasure of his touch. Then he leaned down and licked my slit before taking the bottle of lube and popping the lid. He smeared his hand and fingers liberally, and this time when he gripped me, the slickness of his touch brought with it a whole new level of good.

Then his fingers went lower. He cupped my balls and squeezed gently before going lower still. He slicked my perineum with lube and slowly edged a finger around my arsehole.

"Oh, fuck. Andrew."

He pushed his finger inside me. Just the tip, just enough. Then he pushed a little harder and a little deeper and stroked my cock with his free hand as he fucked me with his finger. When I whined in frustration and pleasure, he added another. Slow at first, but I was soon pushing back onto him, needing more. "Andrew, please. I'm ready."

Then he took me into his mouth, sucking me as he fucked me with his fingers and when he touched something inside me, I saw stars. Then he did it again, and again, and I was lost to it. I gripped the sheets at my side as my orgasm shot through me.

My world went quiet, the room went dark, and my head spun.

I heard a faint chuckle before the sound of foil tearing, and the lid to the lube pop once more. Then he was back between my thighs, pushing my legs up higher and further apart. He leaned over me, his face just above mine, and with his cockhead pressed against my hole, he pushed into me.

He felt so much bigger. *So* much bigger. I watched in wonder as his eyes fluttered closed and his nostrils flared, a picture of such beauty as he breached me. But he was stretching me, slowly, torturously slowly, he was filling me with his huge cock, and when I gasped, his eyes flew open.

He stilled. "Are you okay?" he whispered, his voice hitching as he spoke.

"Fuck," I whined. I inhaled deeply and breathed through the intrusion. "Yes. Keep going. Please."

So he did. But he watched me now, resting on his elbows, his hands at my face. He pushed forward until he was fully seated inside me.

"This," he whispered reverently. His eyes never left mine. "Oh my God, this."

I gasped at the timbre of his voice. Not capable of anything more, I agreed with a nod. "This."

He moved then, thrusting in and out, slow at first and building, faster and deeper, and his eyes squinted closed, and he slid his arms underneath me, holding me tighter. His fingers dug into my body, and he cried out as he stilled over me, inside me.

I grabbed his face and kissed him, plunging my tongue into his mouth as he came. His whole body trembled and shook until he groaned into my mouth and collapsed on me.

All that was left was his hard breaths and the rapid beat of his heart against my chest. He slowly pulled out of me, only to fall on top of me once more. He buried his face in my neck, nuzzled into my beard, and didn't move.

I traced patterns on his back until he sighed. "So worth the wait," he murmured.

I chuckled sleepily. "I agree."

Andrew rolled off me and climbed off the bed. He was gone a moment, disposing of the condom, no doubt. I didn't open my eyes to check. I just held out my arm and waited for him to come back to bed. When he came back, he fit right in against me, like he was designed just for that particular spot, and my arm held him there. "Want me to clean you up a bit?" he asked softly.

"Mm-mm. Nuh." I still hadn't opened my eyes, but I pulled him a bit closer. "Later. Now we sleep."

He settled heavily against me, his head on my shoulder. His breaths soon evened out into a peaceful, deep sleep. I kissed the top of his head and fell asleep, more content and happy than I had felt in a very long time.

I WOKE TO WARM KISSES AND SCRATCHY WHISKERS ON my shoulder. I was lying on my stomach, and there was a delicious weight on my back. "Spencer, wake up."

I smiled into my pillow. "What time is it?"

"Eight o'clock."

"But it's Saturday."

"Exactly." Andrew ran his hands down my back and gripped my hip bones, giving me a jolt of pleasure. "It's Saturday."

I groaned, still half asleep, half really turned on.

He rolled off me and onto the bed beside me. "Guess I'll just have to get my own arse ready."

That made me open my eyes.

He laughed. "That's what I thought."

"You don't play fair." Then I actually looked at him. He was wide awake, smiling, and very fucking naked. He had one knee bent, one hand stroking his dick, and his other hand disappeared down to where I imagined he was playing with his own arse. "Jesus."

"I woke up with your dick against my ass," he said. "So this is technically your fault."

I barked out a laugh and rolled onto my back, the sheet half coming off my side. My morning wood had become fully fledged wood and I couldn't help but palm myself. "I'll happily take the blame for that." But morning was morning, and I needed to take a piss. I got off the bed and stretched, giving Andrew a full, shameless eyeful.

He licked his lips and bit back a moan. I laughed, and he scowled at me. "Hurry up!"

I laughed as I walked into the steamy bathroom. "Did you shower already?" I called out as I relieved myself. It was never easy urinating with an erection.

"Yeah. Hope you don't mind."

I washed my hands and my face and walked back into my room. He was still splayed out on the bed, his thick long cock now lying across his hip. It stopped me where I stood.

He smiled. "I figured I'd, you know, get myself ready and cleaned up for you."

I looked behind me, like I was searching for something. "Have you seen shy Andrew anywhere? I seem to have misplaced him. Sexy Andrew is still here, and demanding Andrew is here, but that shy, blushing Andrew seems to have disappeared."

He chuckled. "I'm not really shy. Awkward sometimes and easily embarrassed but not shy. If I want something, I will ask for it. Is that okay?"

I knelt on the bed at his feet. "That is more than okay. So tell me what you want."

"I want you to rim me, then fuck me."

Jesus Christ. His words set fire to my blood. "Fuck Andrew," I mumbled, giving my dick a squeeze. "You'll make me come if you talk like that."

He smiled like he'd just accepted that as a challenge, but he didn't say anything. He just casually stroked himself, waiting for instruction.

"Roll over," I ordered. "Put the pillows under your hips."

He did, and his perfect arse was perched up and waiting. Fuck. I spread his legs a little wider and knelt between them. I put my hands to his arse cheeks, spreading them, and nuzzled my beard against the sensitive skin around his hole.

He hummed in anticipation, so I let my hot breath wash over his entrance, knowing the different sensations only heightened the experience. He groaned, impatient and wanting. He was so turned on, and he loved being eaten out.

"Mmm, breakfast of champions," I said.

He laughed into the mattress, and that was when I licked over his hole. His laughter caught, strangled in his throat, overtaken by a sound of unsolicited pleasure. He gripped the sheets and raised his hips. So I spread him a little wider, and slipped my tongue inside him, making him gasp and moan.

The more I did it, the more he wanted, pushing back to meet me, and it wasn't long until he was thrusting and rutting into the pillows while I fucked his arse with my tongue.

"Spencer, I really need you," he ground out. His voice was desperate. "Need you inside me. More, need more."

I found a condom and slicked myself up with lube and

added more to his waiting and ready arse. He was still on his stomach, his arse in the air; his breathing was sharp and desperate.

I positioned myself over him, my cock at his hole and gently pressed into him. He was so warm and tight, so slick and welcoming. His shoulder muscles bulged as he fisted the bedcovers, but he kept his arse high and his head down. "Fuuuuuuuuck," he groaned the word.

I pushed in slowly, all the way, and gave him time to adjust. And for me to calm down. I'd never felt this connection. More emotional than physical, the need to show him how I felt was more important than fucking.

And in that moment, I understood what it meant to make love. I'd always thought of it as fucking or sex. The physical need for release, the primal urge to claim and own, to give and receive pleasure.

But this was so different. Each movement was tender, timed with his breaths. Each thrust was in sync with my heart, and I held him. I slid my hands under his shoulders and held him as I filled him. I kissed the back of his neck, scraping my teeth against his skin, and when I couldn't hold the tide of pleasure back any longer, I simply let it go.

When my world came back to me, I was still inside him.

My heart beat in time with his, our pulses united.

I slowly pulled out but stayed where I was. I kissed the back of his neck again and murmured his name. "Andrew."

"You okay?" he asked.

I'd just had a huge, monumental moment in my life. Not just the acknowledgment that I was in love with him, but the realisation I was capable of such a powerful emotion, such an all-encompassing, soul-rendering emotion. And, that I was deserving of it too. Something years of therapy hadn't quite managed to convince me of, Andrew did it in a matter of weeks. Not that I could tell him that. Not yet, anyway.

"I'm more than okay," I answered. I rolled off him but kept him in my arms. "Can we go back to sleep now?"

He chuckled but shook his head against my chest. "Nope." Then he sidled up, fully against me, letting me feel his still-hard cock. "Your work isn't done."

I laughed. "I was selfish, sorry."

"You were so hot," he said. "Don't apologise because that was pretty damn amazing."

"But you didn't come."

"Not yet, anyway."

"I'd like you to."

He ground his hips against me. "Where?"

"Wherever you want."

Andrew groaned, and peeling himself away from me, he got to his knees on the bed beside me. "Open your mouth."

Smiling, I shoved a pillow under my neck, opened my mouth, and flattened my tongue, ready for his cock. He certainly didn't waste his time, and I didn't waste a drop.

WE SLEPT SOME MORE, WE SHOWERED, WE ATE, WE laughed. We listened to the piano concerto album he bought me the other day, and Andrew spent a good while trying to figure out how we could possibly have sex in the papasan chair. He changed his Facebook status to "In a relationship" and we added a selfie of us laughing on the couch and he got a gazillion likes and questions, but he turned his phone off and slid it onto the coffee table. I spoke to Peter Hannikov, my prospective new client, and arranged to see him Monday. After which, my phone joined Andrew's on the coffee table.

Andrew pulled me back onto the sofa and kissed the side of my head. We watched *A Clockwork Orange*, all cuddled up, which inevitably led to more sex.

He was insatiable.

And wonderful.

We eventually made an appearance downstairs in the shop at dinner time, only staying long enough for a few crude jokes at our just-had-sex expense, and to offer to get anyone something to eat. Then, still laughing, Andrew took my hand and pulled me out into the warm LA night.

We walked hand in hand down the street, and it was truly the happiest and freest I could remember being. Andrew led the way to the Moroccan restaurant and held the door open for me. Zineb greeted us with a clap of her hands and a huge smile, like we were her two prodigal sons. "Oh, I not see you in so long," she cried. "Come sit, let me get you tea."

She disappeared, and not a moment later, she came back with a pot of green tea and two cups. One for me, one for Andrew. "Oh, I don't drink that—" Andrew started to say.

Zineb put her hand up, stopping him. "You drink it."

"Okay," he said quickly.

I laughed and Zineb looked at me fondly. "Oh, my Spencer. Look at you. There is happiness in your eyes." She looked up to the ceiling as if in prayer. "Finally." Then she leaned down, and taking a hold of Andrew's face, she kissed the top of his head. "Thank you, thank you."

Andrew blushed and shrank back in his chair, but all I could do was smile. I poured him a tea, then one for myself. I held my cup and waited for him to do the same so I could clink my cup to his. I sighed happily. "I'd like to buy you something tonight, when we leave here," I told him.

"Oh yeah? What's that?" He sipped the tea and considered it thoughtfully for a moment. "I'm not sure what you can possibly get me that will beat the record player or albums or the coolest book ever written."

"It's better than all those things."

He looked at me like I was crazy. "How can it possibly be better than those things? Unless you found an actual copy of *Living Sexy in LA* with you on the cover, I don't think it's possible."

I laughed at him. "I was thinking I could buy you a toothbrush. You know, for my place."

He stared.

"I know we said we'd hold off on buying them. I know what it represents, and I know you're worried about rushing into things," I added quickly. He was still staring. "But if it's all right with you, I think I'd like to take that step. I mean, it's just a toothbrush."

His smile was slow spreading, a faint blush tinted his cheeks and warmth filled his eyes. "I'd like that."

I felt like I'd just confessed my love for him, not just the promise of a stupid toothbrush. It was ridiculous how happy and nervous it made me. But after we ate, we made our way to the store and bought a tub of lemon gelato, and two toothbrushes.

One for me at his place, and one for him at mine.

The End

ABOUT THE AUTHOR

N.R. Walker is an Australian author, who loves her genre of gay romance. She loves writing and spends far too much time doing it, but wouldn't have it any other way.

She is many things: a mother, a wife, a sister, a writer. She has pretty, pretty boys who live in her head, who don't let her sleep at night unless she gives them life with words.

She likes it when they do dirty, dirty things… but likes it even more when they fall in love.

She used to think having people in her head talking to her was weird, until one day she happened across other writers who told her it was normal.

She's been writing ever since…

ALSO BY N.R. WALKER

Blind Faith

Through These Eyes (Blind Faith #2)

Blindside: Mark's Story (Blind Faith #3)

Ten in the Bin

Gay Sex Club Stories 1

Gay Sex Club Stories 2

Point of No Return – Turning Point #1

Breaking Point – Turning Point #2

Starting Point – Turning Point #3

Element of Retrofit – Thomas Elkin Series #1

Clarity of Lines – Thomas Elkin Series #2

Sense of Place – Thomas Elkin Series #3

Taxes and TARDIS

Three's Company

Red Dirt Heart

Red Dirt Heart 2

Red Dirt Heart 3

Red Dirt Heart 4

Red Dirt Christmas

Cronin's Key

Cronin's Key II

Cronin's Key III

Cronin's Key IV - Kennard's Story

Exchange of Hearts

The Spencer Cohen Series, Book One

The Spencer Cohen Series, Book Two

The Spencer Cohen Series, Book Three

The Spencer Cohen Series, Yanni's Story

Blood & Milk

The Weight Of It All

A Very Henry Christmas (The Weight of It All 1.5)

Perfect Catch

Switched

Imago

Imagines

Imagoes

Red Dirt Heart Imago

On Davis Row

Finders Keepers

Evolved

Galaxies and Oceans

Private Charter

Nova Praetorian

A Soldier's Wish

Upside Down

The Hate You Drink

Sir

Tallowwood

Reindeer Games

The Dichotomy of Angels

Throwing Hearts

Pieces of You - Missing Pieces #1

Pieces of Me - Missing Pieces #2

Pieces of Us - Missing Pieces #3

Lacuna

Tic-Tac-Mistletoe

Bossy

Code Red

Dearest Milton James

Dearest Malachi Keogh

Christmas Wish List

Code Blue

Davo

The Kite

Learning Curve

Merry Christmas Cupid

To the Moon and Back

TITLES IN AUDIO:

Cronin's Key

Cronin's Key II

Cronin's Key III

Red Dirt Heart

Red Dirt Heart 2

Red Dirt Heart 3

Red Dirt Heart 4

The Weight Of It All

Switched

Point of No Return

Breaking Point

Starting Point

Spencer Cohen Book One

Spencer Cohen Book Two

Spencer Cohen Book Three

Yanni's Story

On Davis Row

Evolved

Elements of Retrofit

Clarity of Lines

Sense of Place

Blind Faith

Through These Eyes

Blindside

Finders Keepers

Galaxies and Oceans

Nova Praetorian

Upside Down

Sir

Tallowwood

Imago

Throwing Hearts

Sixty Five Hours

Taxes and TARDIS

The Dichotomy of Angels

The Hate You Drink

Pieces of You

Pieces of Me

Pieces of Us

Tic-Tac-Mistletoe

Lacuna

Bossy

Code Red

Learning to Feel

Dearest Milton James

Dearest Malachi Keogh

Three's Company

Christmas Wish List

Code Blue

Davo

The Kite

Learning Curve

Merry Christmas Cupid

To the Moon and Back

SERIES COLLECTIONS:

Red Dirt Heart Series

Turning Point Series

Thomas Elkin Series

Spencer Cohen Series

Imago Series

Blind Faith Series

FREE READS:

Sixty Five Hours

Learning to Feel

His Grandfather's Watch (And The Story of Billy and Hale)

The Twelfth of Never (Blind Faith 3.5)

Twelve Days of Christmas (Sixty Five Hours Christmas)

Best of Both Worlds

TRANSLATED TITLES:

ITALIAN

Fiducia Cieca (Blind Faith)

Attraverso Questi Occhi (Through These Eyes)

Preso alla Sprovvista (Blindside)

Il giorno del Mai (Blind Faith 3.5)

Cuore di Terra Rossa Serie (Red Dirt Heart Series)

Natale di terra rossa (Red dirt Christmas)

Intervento di Retrofit (Elements of Retrofit)

A Chiare Linee (Clarity of Lines)

Senso D'appartenenza (Sense of Place)

Spencer Cohen Serie (including Yanni's Story)

Punto di non Ritorno (Point of No Return)

Punto di Rottura (Breaking Point)

Punto di Partenza (Starting Point)

Imago (Imago)

Il desiderio di un soldato (A Soldier's Wish)

Scambiato (Switched)

Galassie e Oceani (Galaxies and Oceans)

FRENCH

Confiance Aveugle (Blind Faith)

A travers ces yeux: Confiance Aveugle 2 (Through These Eyes)

Aveugle: Confiance Aveugle 3 (Blindside)

À Jamais (Blind Faith 3.5)

Cronin's Key Series

Au Coeur de Sutton Station (Red Dirt Heart)

Partir ou rester (Red Dirt Heart 2)

Faire Face (Red Dirt Heart 3)

Trouver sa Place (Red Dirt Heart 4)

Le Poids de Sentiments (The Weight of It All)

Un Noël à la sauce Henry (A Very Henry Christmas)

Une vie à Refaire (Switched)

Evolution (Evolved)

Galaxies & Océans

Qui Trouve, Garde (Finders Keepers)

Sens Dessus Dessous (Upside Down)

Spencer Cohen Series

GERMAN

Flammende Erde (Red Dirt Heart)

Lodernde Erde (Red Dirt Heart 2)

Sengende Erde (Red Dirt Heart 3)

Ungezähmte Erde (Red Dirt Heart 4)

Vier Pfoten und ein bisschen Zufall (Finders Keepers)

Ein Kleines bisschen Versuchung (The Weight of It All)

Ein Kleines Bisschen Fur Immer (A Very Henry Christmas)

Weil Leibe uns immer Bliebt (Switched)

Drei Herzen eine Leibe (Three's Company)

Über uns die Sterne, zwischen uns die Liebe (Galaxies and Oceans)

Unnahbares Herz (Blind Faith 1)

Sehendes Herz (Blind Faith 2)

Hoffnungsvolles Herz (Blind Faith 3)

Verträumtes Herz (Blind Faith 3.5)

Thomas Elkin: Verlangen in neuem Design

Traummann töpfern leicht gemacht (Throwing Hearts)

THAI

Sixty Five Hours (Thai translation)

Finders Keepers (Thai translation)

SPANISH

Sesenta y Cinco Horas (Sixty Five Hours)

Los Doce Días de Navidad

Código Rojo (Code Red)

Código Azul (Code Blue)

Queridísimo Milton James

Queridísimo Malachi Keogh

El Peso de Todo (The Weight of it All)

Tres Muérdagos en Raya: Serie Navidad en Hartbridge

Lista De Deseos Navideños: Serie Navidad en Hartbridge

Spencer Cohen Libro Uno

Spencer Cohen Libro Dos

Spencer Cohen Libro Tres

La Historia de Yanni

Davo

Feliz Navidad Cupido: Serie Navidad en Hartbridge

CHINESE

Blind Faith

www.ingramcontent.com/pod-product-compliance
Lightning Source LLC
Chambersburg PA
CBHW050528190726
48284CB00003B/983